A Good Hater

Frederick Boyle

Contents

A GOOD HATER

BY

Frederick Boyle

A GOOD HATER.

CHAPTER I.
OUR HEEOES.

THERE is no district in London, I think, so gracefully respectable as Eaton Square. That address suggests a mediocrity which is golden in every sense—disdainful of pretension on one side, and of dull dignity on the other. And a typical house therein was Mrs. Acland's, small but airy, broad of window, high of ceiling; its few rooms equally convenient for receiving a score of chosen guests, and comfortable for the family. Taste bad directed the expenditure of a vast amount of cash in furnishing them. There was no crowding of objects, and no display; but somehow, if a visitor looked in any direction with an observing eye, he saw something unusual—a very small matter, perhaps, but one that pleased him. It was declared by many persons who speak with authority, that no dwelling in London, positively none, was so perfect in every detail. And not a few would have liked to add, if they dared, that the ladies therein were most consummate of all.

Although Mrs. Acland was treated by everybody as the owner—that is to say, the lessee—of this delightful house, it belonged in reality to her son since he came of age, and before that event to his trustees. But Hugh had never asserted nor even recognised his rights against his mother. All the world esteemed and liked and respected Mrs. Acland, but her children idolized her. A woman of large but most shapely frame, her features, too pronounced for the word 'pretty,' but too soft for 'handsome,' could only be described as charming. The laugh was always ready to her dark eyes; not the laugh of complacency or of feeble good-nature, but shrewd as kind. Neither she nor her children had known a day's illness in their lives.

A very picture of intelligent ease and graceful happiness was this lady; but she had gone through trouble, as was generally known. Her husband was drowned before he came into the estate of Worstan, which now belonged to his son, and for some years the widow had to live upon a meagre allowance. She made no secret of her bitter experience—Mrs. Acland had no secrets—but she alluded to it only, with laughing tact, as her excuse for a broad and charitable knowledge of the world which might be thought to need explanation among dames of a certain standing. An abstract acquaintance with human nature and an abstract consideration for its weakness are expected of everyone nowadays; but Mrs. Acland's views upon the matter were decidedly practical. Servants alone regarded her with distrust; not because she was unkind, for nobody could show more indulgence, but because she saw through them with such good-natured keenness, understood so well what, ought or ought not to be overlooked, made up her mind so inexorably, and was always right. In brief, a woman fascinating in the best sense, a companion cultured and interesting, a judicious adviser, a warm friend, and, if need be, a cool and resolute antagonist.

Of her children, Hugh, the elder, had not quite entered his twenty-fourth year at this date, the prologue of our story. I need not speak of his character, but it may be said that a mother so reasonable as Mrs. Acland would hardly have hoped, even though she had wished, to have it better than it was. Hugh had gone through the training proper for a man of family and means and station, with such credit as is fitting, without scandal, but not without such little adventures as gentlemen of the old school think becoming to young blood. If he passed not an inch beyond—seeing that the boy had spirit, fine health, and quite a sufficient proportion of conceit—it may be that his mother's influence saved him unconsciously. She knew the temptations that beset golden youth, and she warned her son, not by grave precept, nor by argument, still less by appeal. Hers was a better way, which all parents cannot follow, unhappily. She told stories that made Hugh laugh, but pointed a moral all the sharper and all the more enduring because they left him to draw it for himself. And so he passed without damage through the years of greatest danger to the freshness of his heart, and to the accumulations of a long minority. One could not find a blither young fellow in town, nor a catch more desirable to parents who considered the happiness of their daughter; nor one more difficult to secure, whilst he confided all inclinations of that grave sort to his mother.

The other child was Edith, eighteen years old on December 10th next, but commonly granted at least a twelvemonth more, because she had been 'brought out' at a very early age. In her one recognised at a glance the beauty which had distracted her mother's contemporaries; the exquisite shape, rounded as a woman's but slender as a girl's, the features perfect though 'unclassical,' the large eyes full of intelligence; but not the expression. Mrs. Acland's real experiences of life had taught her cheerfulness and charity. "When no one could be spying, her air was still quick with such easy enjoyment of life as an untroubled conscience and happy circumstances bring to a sound digestion. Edie could laugh with a glee more cheerful than her years, and very often did; but depression seized her when alone. The girl's nature was thoughtful and self-questioning. Had she been less strong of constitution, she would probably have felt 'a call' or a craze. Perceiving this, Mrs. Acland, always practical, introduced her to society at an age much earlier than is common. Edie was several months under sixteen when she began to accompany her mother to balls and parties; but no one suspected her youth, and in the circles, not unimportant, where they moved, Miss Acland was a reigning beauty from the outset. Her triumph was complete and immediate, but it had not the effect upon her which had been desired. Up to a certain point, Edie felt interested in gaieties, dress, partners and the rest, but the point never moved. Mrs. Acland watched her daughter more anxiously, for low spirits in a girl seemed to her cheerful disposition a very grave portent. She began to think with distress that an early marriage was desirable; but Edie did not share this view evidently, for she had checked several young men whose attentions were welcome in the highest quarters.

This report must not be misunderstood, however. It is strictly confidential, giving the state of things in Mrs. Acland's house-hold not as the world saw it, but as it really was. No two opinions were current, indeed, about the lady herself; her open and lively disposition, her good sense, and pleasant humour spoke for themselves. But people were apt to think Hugh more bumptious than he really was; and for Edie, they declared her to be the very nicest girl that' such a beauty could be—a little too grave, perhaps, but gravity sat so charmingly on her intelligent face—a little too clever, possibly, but so unaffected with it all! And the world was unanimous that another family so blest in every way could not be found in Britain. Which was the reasoned opinion of Mrs. Acland herself.

The companion picture represents a snowy plain beneath the Khojak Amram Mountains, in Afghanistan. Battery X 3, R.A., is encamped there, with its escort of Sepoys, returning to India. The day has been very hot, and round the tents the snow is melted and trampled into puddles; but the coming frost has begun, and men throng round the fires, clad in their sheepskins. Officers stump up and down before the mess-tent, eagerly awaiting the bugle, which will not sound for half an hour; but in their tents it is deadly cold, and the solitary candle is depressing. One of them, however, is writing within; his shadow falls blurred upon the canvas.

'. . . In a few weeks we hope to be in the old quarters at Meerut, and we call it going "home." The word unsettles me. When shall I see you and my real home again? They say I have a fair chance of promotion, and—one does not mind talking nonsense to one's mother—of honours you will value more. If the promotion comes off, I fondly think I will apply for leave at last! How the eternal difficulty about cash is to be got over I have no idea at all, but the mere thought cheers one on this dreariest of campaigns. I vow the snow of Scarsholme is warmer than that round my tent now.

'Talking of home and you, mother, naturally brings Grace to my mind—when I have time to think, indeed, those three subjects turn about in my mind with a regularity almost disconcerting to a man who has so many other things to think of. Grace's letter acknowledging the photograph reached me at Cabul, and I've worn a smile off duty ever since—unfortunately we are so seldom off duty that the men persist in regarding me as a grave and serious personage. Tell me confidentially, mother, what Grace said. She must have been startled. I looked at my own likeness very long, very many times, before sending it, and at the glass, too. Somehow I do not recognise the lank face which they both show as *mine.* I don't own it, and I don't feel it as my property, though I have too much reason to believe that the impostor has established a general impression that he is the real and the only Captain Richard Saxell in her Majesty's Artillery service. Don't repeat this nonsense to Grace, but tell me what she said at the first glimpse of the photograph. I think I understand her well enough to know that *that* impression will recur and abide. . . .

'You complain that I give so little detail of our life in the field. I have really had few adventures. A battle in these times is no personal affair, so to speak, especially for a gunner. When you read that Battery X 3 took part in an engagement, you know that Captain Saxell was there, doing his duty as well as he knows how. And Captain Saxell can tell you little more. I have had only one bit of adventure since the campaign began. It was in the action of Abdallah-Karez, which you read of. The Ghilzai Ghazis charged us suddenly, breaking the line of infantry. We limbered up to withdraw, but the last gun stuck, and before it could be got out fifty of them were on us. We made the best fight possible, but our men are unarmed—that is, they allow us only twenty-five carbines to a battery, and small blame to those who decline to meet a Pathan knife with a whip! Such as had carbines stood their ground, and the gun was brought away. We went after it helter-skelter. I thought all had got off, until some one cried that Sergeant-Major Raikes was missing. I looked back. The Ghilzais were chasing us in a crowd, but a number of them clustered round a pony, on which they were trying to lift something. The 30th B. C. charged at that moment, and we had the good fortune to rescue poor Raikes, little hurt. He is very grateful. I must tell you about our sergeant-major some day, as we sit round the fire at home and Grace asks for stories. He is an odd fellow——There goes the mess-bugle—not too soon, for my ink is frozen. We shall reach Chaman to-morrow, where I shall post this, and expect letters from you and Grace. Our route is not through the Khojak Pass, but through the Guaja. This detour will cause some delay., so you will not be surprised if my next is somewhat behindhand.'

Three days later Captain Saxell wrote to another correspondent:

'In the Guaja Pass, Nov. 25.

'DEAR VANE,

'I found your letter of October 1st at Chaman. It has distressed me much—more even than you thought. I had been cherishing hopes which must now be thrown aside. When I think of the shifts to which poverty compels my poor mother, I feel hopelessly enraged against Fate. My brain has been working incessantly to devise some fresh saving, which might enable me to remit even £20, but I can think of none. I shall write to Grace frankly this mail. It is not right she should be tied to a pauper who is verging on the fogey at twenty-nine years old. If I have been deceiving myself, I hope I have not been deceiving Grace—and I think not. We have both regarded it as a vision. If it were realized, I should be the happiest fellow living—or, at least, as happy as the best; and Grace perhaps would pay me the same compliment. But it cannot be realized, Vane, so far as I see. If my majority was posted in the next ***Gazette,*** it would make no effectual difference. After all, a girl of eighteen cannot seriously feel the breaking of an engagement with a man whom she has not beheld for nine years—or close on it. For the rest, I can do nothing! Would it be impossible for my mother to engage one of those "lady helps" we read of as a house-keeper? With her own income, Grace's allowance, and the money I remit, she has means which would be wealth to some ladies. Management is lacking. . . .

'Our situation here is not one to raise the spirits. We are snowed up in the Guaja Pass—on the right side, fortunately. The great cliffs, where a child with a crowbar could crush a regiment, lie behind us. I cannot believe there is another scene in the world like that. Imagine a road only fifty feet in width, overhung by mountains that rise just like a wall on either side I don't know how many hundreds of feet high, vast rents and cracks intersecting them. Rocks as big as a house are poised above one's head, so cut and riven that it seems a breath of wind would bring them down. And think also in what country we were travelling! At a giddy height, no bigger than birds, the Kakar scouts looked down on us. We saw them climbing and gesticulating, their white felt robes sparkling in the sunshine, whilst we crept on in twilight. Men scarcely spoke, but toiled along with eyes upraised, expecting every step to be their last. That fright is over, thank Heaven! By sunset yesterday we reached this small amphitheatre in the defile, and thought our troubles past.

'But when I woke in the dull grey dawn, our camp was buried in snow. It lies a foot deep even on the hills, and if the wind rises we may be almost smothered in drift. Things are very serious, for we have but six days' fodder. However, you will hear the end long before this reaches you. We are escorted, as you know, by six companies of the 130th N. I. Our Pathan Sepoys are particularly lively, but all the rest lie torpid with cold. Even the Sikhs are helpless; when spoken to they look up with great eyes and drawn features, but do not move. Our servants simply want to die in peace, and I expect that a good many of them will find their prayer granted before morning. My Pathan grass-cutter has dug a hole in the middle of the tent, which he keeps full of charcoal, and so I am able to write, thawing my hand every five minutes. To talk to you, old friend, distracts my thoughts.

'To a painter's eye, I suppose our camp would be mighty picturesque. It lies in a small valley just below the Kotul, the head of the pass. Those lofty cliffs I spoke of seem to overhang it in the rear. The gains are ranged across, pointing forwards—a bad disposition if we are attacked from the rear, but the men were worn out last night, as were officers indeed. Our stained and ragged tents look more discreditable than ever against the pure white of the snow. It lies so deep that most of the stunted bushes are hidden beneath it, and the jagged hillsides slant smoothly down. There are fine pista-trees about, gnarled, grey old stumps, with heads like a thousand snakes, writhing and fighting. We hear scarce a sound in camp, but ravens croak incessantly as they flap from hill to hill, and starved partridges twitter in the snow.

'The Major summoned me to council as I was writing the last line. It seems that an Afridi Sepoy casually remarked to one of his officers that the Kakars are sure to attack. Examined by the Colonel, he says a Kakar Sepoy told him so, and the Kakar cheerfully admits the prophecy. He ought to know the ways of his own people, so we have been doing what we can to prepare. Guns have been turned by main force to command the flanks, but we found it impossible to take up a new position. It will be necessary to strike the pal tents if the enemy really comes. When all has been done our situation will be very ugly, commanded as it is on every side within easy range of a jezail. However, it's as God wills—we are doing our best. The camp is busy enough now. Men relieve each other with the spade, clearing broad paths to the hills by which our pickets can be reinforced without delay, and raising sungas. I have run in to warm my feet whilst the men take their dinner.

'8 p.m.

'No sign of the enemy all day, and they cannot approach us in the dark. I must tell you a very odd thing. I was seated on a fallen pista-tree, superintending a gang of men. The sergeant-major of the battery was beside me, and we spoke of the measures to be taken in case of attack. Raikes, I must tell you, is a very old soldier, who has evidently known better days; in fact, he is an educated man, and a gentleman by birth, one can see that. He took a gloomy view of things. At last he said, "I should like to speak with you, sir, after work's done." I consented, of course; I can't tell you all he said, but it came to this:

'Our poor sergeant-major married young; his wife deceived him; he enlisted and came to India, leaving such indications as made people suppose him dead. Some short time afterwards a considerable property devolved upon him or his heirs. He did not hear of the fact for a long while, and then he took no steps. His son inherited, he supposes. But now Raikes has made a will, which, as he declares, leaves everything he can dispose of to somebody else, and he asked me to take charge of it.

'Such requests are common enough when a soldier has some trifle to dispose of, but this case is different. The sergeant-major talks as if he were a rich man. The people his will disinherits won't thank me. I asked who they were, and he said they were his wife and a daughter, whom he does not acknowledge. The son also, in part, I suppose.

'I plainly pointed out that the commission was not agreeable, but he insisted. One does not like to refuse a service in front of the enemy, and Raikes has a sort of claim upon me. So, after dinner he came with his witnesses and gave me the document sealed up, in the presence of St. Paul, our Major. I resolved to write an account of the transaction while it was fresh in my mind. . . . .

'Mahmoud Khan-ka-Killah, Nov. 28.

'Through the defile, as you see, and myself little hurt; but too many of our poor fellows are left behind. When the bugle sounded at dawn on the 26th snow was falling softly. The men drank their tea and mustered for fatigue-duty. The snow fell thicker. I had crossed to the native lines, where the Pathan Sepoys were working cheerily, as many as could get shovels. I saw them pause, listening. There was such a clang of tools and hearty English voices where I stood with the Colonel that we could hear nothing else. Suddenly, they ran towards their tents. I ordered our men to cease working, and dead silence followed, except a faint clash of arms where the Pathans had vanished. Then in the distance, high overhead, where hill-tops loomed unseen in mist and driving snow, we heard a ringing chorus. In long-drawn notes it swelled and sank, to burst out in a new direction, till every slope and crag around us echoed.

' "Sound to arms, trumpeter!" cried Colonel Blair, running. Before he reached the tents, his gallant fellows were mustering, the Pathans noisy and excited, the Sikhs shivering but steady. As the native bagpipes screamed, and the drums rattled, we heard no reply up above. The song had ceased abruptly when its purpose was answered in showing the surround complete.

'Our dispositions were already settled. The high ground immediately about our camp was held by pickets, as large as our strength would bear. The danger lay in a rush of overwhelming numbers, who might get within charging-distance under cover of the snow, which fell heavily. Sentries had been pushed out as far as was safe, and the ground surveyed overnight. Colonel Blair sent off parties at the double to reinforce the pickets, and to occupy the sungas we had built. Within a few moments the firing began, dropping shots at first, which multiplied and thickened till we stood in a ring of fire, though not a flash was to be seen. Colonel Blair walked anxiously up and down before the three companies of Sepoys remaining in camp. The doctors were preparing a field hospital under a tree, round which lay dhoolies ranged in a circle, the bearers squatting amongst them. Some had lit their hubble-bubbles for a last smoke.

'In such a fight gunners are helpless. We had loaded with grape, armed the drivers, and then we could but wait events. Wounded men came straggling from the pickets. Then bullets began to spit and whizz among us, showing that the enemy was creeping nearer. Half a company of Sepoys, young Birt at their head, doubled off and vanished. The firing had slackened in the quarter to which they went, but it broke out more fiercely, and crackled without pause.

'That was a terrible fifteen minutes. Then the fall of snow began to cease. We could see ten yards—twenty. The flash of musketry and the sharp puffs of smoke became visible, but dim and indistinct. Our pickets still held their own, but the ragged flags were tossing perilously near them. Only an instant I looked. A shout from the Major drew all our eyes away. At fifty yards' distance, grey-robed figures came pouring from the rock itself, scores of them, one upon another. "Fire!" At that range grape sped like a solid shot, but ricocheting from the cliff it dropped the foremost in a heap. Before another gun could he discharged, we were fighting hand to hand. The Sepoys poured in to our support with fixed bayonets, their clear old Colonel at their head. The Pathans had only swords, but yelling their "Allah-hu!" eyes aflame, hair streaming, giant bodies half-stripped, they took the guns with a rush. It was an awful tussle, Vane! We were driven back among the tents before the Sepoys reached us. Enemy and friend tripped over the ropes, and fought on the miry ground. When the soldiers pushed through, forcing back the rush, wounded Pathans caught them by the leg and dragged them down, biting and stabbing. Raikes, our sergeant-major, fell like that; and before I could rescue him the Kakar devil had twice run him through, holding his right hand in his teeth. But our Sepoys pressed on, and a flank attack cleared the ground. Most of the Pathans fell where they stood. As the last of the fugitives vanished, a burst of "Allah-hu!" told that one of our pickets was overwhelmed. But the enemy saw the failure of their main attack, and they did not follow up. After firing a volley into camp, and murdering the wounded, they withdrew. We pitched some shells haphazard, and all was over.

'Our losses are heavy, and of those not mortally wounded a large proportion will die of wet and cold, and misery. It was dreadful to hear the cry of brave men that night. At sunset came a thaw, but it brought them no ease. A south wind melted the snow all night, and the sun rose furiously hot. Before noon the road was a muddy torrent, every slope a quagmire. We had not dhoolies enough for the wounded, but to stay was death for all. I say nothing—I shall never bear to speak of that march. Fancy yourself helpless amidst all the horrors of despair and agony that one could laboriously imagine! We buried nine before starting, six more by the roadside; their dhoolies were re-occupied before they had grown cold. By evening we were not clear of the pass, and we camped in the mud, under heavy rain. Nine deaths in the night, and five on the morning's march. We have sent to Quettah for aid. I expect to arrive there in about a week, and I will keep this open for the latest news.

'Quettah, Dec. 8.

'The latest news is startling. Poor Raikes died this afternoon, but you will not see at a glance how that affects me.

'I gave him as much time as I could, since he continually asked for me. There was no hope, and Raikes did not deceive himself. I never saw a man, who confessed that his life had been godless, so perfectly cool and determined. He told me in outline at various times a good deal of his story, which was sad enough, but generally he did not pretend to have merited better fortune. A desperately bad man, I should think, who had naturally fallen into bad society.

'Our sergeant-major's real name was Acland, and he was heir to a good estate— Worstan. I think I have heard of that place. He supposed that in due course it fell to him, and that it is now in possession of his son. Acland made an unhappy marriage when very young. His wife deceived him with a man named Beaver, after the son's birth. His father had cut him off on account of the marriage, and his circumstances were quite desperate. He avenged himself on Beaver by knocking him down in his own park, and beating him until he was left for dead, then carried out a scheme which made people believe him drowned;—went away to London, and enlisted as John Raikes. From that clay he held no communication with his family.

'Worstan was owned by an uncle, with whom he was never on bad terms, but an ill-conditioned sort of fellow;—like all of his race indeed, as Acland suggests. At the death of this uncle his father would succeed. One or both may be living now, for they were both excellent lives, but the chances are against it, of course. If they are dead, the boy has Worstan probably. You will soon see what a strong motive I have for telling you all this.

'The uncle once told him, after a quarrel with his father, that he should leave him all the personalty, a large sum. Acland, or Raikes, has no doubt that he did so, if the old man is dead. And that personalty, whatever it be, is left by will to *myself!*

'It has been inherited, Acland supposes, by his wife, son, and reputed daughter, if they are alive, or by their heirs. I can hardly trust myself yet to discuss the matter.

'This morning the last change came, and he sent for Major St. Paul, who commands our battery, myself, and Sergeant Atkins, the surviving witness of his will. He asked me to bring the paper, broke the seals, and begged St. Paul to read it aloud. You may fancy my astonishment. I urged him to think again, pointing out that I had no rights, and so on. He declared that I had saved his life once, and had tried to do so a second time; that his son was provided for; as to his wife and the daughter whom he disowned, they had no claim to consideration. One cannot argue at length with a dying man. After many words, I said that under all the circumstances T would not refuse; but I flatly declined to commit myself further, though you know how great my temptation is.

'Acland saw me hesitate, I suppose, and he added a codicil there and then, which you will observe. It forbids me to compromise with his widow, or whoever it may be, and declares if I entertain such a notion, or refuse to accept the legacy, my rights pass to my mother, under the same stipulation; and in case of her declining, the money is left to Chelsea Hospital. It was clear that Acland was influenced as much by malice towards his wife as by gratitude towards me, and, though it was painful to speak sharply, I could not forbear to say as much. He answered: "We're good haters in our family, sir, and we mostly die in a dreadful frame of mind. But it isn't only that. I've made a resolution to leave you, who saved my life, what I have justly to dispose of; and I know just as well as I know that I am dying, how *she'll* make a fool of an honest man like you. The years I passed with her taught me something of the cool wicked ness a clever, taking woman will practise for sport; and Margaret will have all her interests at stake here. As sure as you're alive, Saxell, or as I'm nearly dead, she'll deceive you somehow. If you believe me, and fight out the case, she'll contrive that some doubts shall haunt you. But I don't expect you will be able to resist the clever tricks. She will turn you round her finger, and make you so uncomfortable that you'll be glad to accept some small amount and let the matter drop, or else you'll refuse altogether. That I don't mean to submit to. Mrs. Saxell may be less trusting, and any way she's a woman. If I'm wrong about her, the Governors of Chelsea Hospital can't be wheedled. That's how it is!"

'He had spoken with great force, and lie dropped back exhausted. Then the chaplain came, and we left him. The man died suddenly in my arms just as I returned. Davies, our chaplain, tells me that he did not speak again.

'Now, what am I to do about it? As regards the value of the will and codicil in law, that is a matter for you to examine. But I know that judges are very tolerant of irregularity in form when the testator was a man killed in the service of his country. I put that question aside.

'It is not to be doubted that Acland wished to revenge himself upon his wife;— we call him Acland, you see, because St. Paul agrees with me that his manner and bearing towards the last are quite consonant with his story so far. And it is not to be assumed that a man who knew he was dying would tell a falsehood. There is the possibility that he spoke under an hallucination. That, in the first place, would seem improbable from what I personally knew of Raikes. None of us, officers or comrades, would believe it without medical authority or clear proof. He was not popular, but the men respected him, and we all put confidence in our sergeant-major. There are, I gather now, some vague traditions of his having broken loose; but they refer to several years back, when he was serving in P. 2. Since we have known him in this battery he has been a quiet, self-contained, trustworthy soldier, not likely to be given to illusions. And St. Paul is just as well satisfied as myself that this tale is no sudden fancy. As to that, we shall know more when his effects are overhauled at Meerut. He has authorized me to take possession of them, and to make any use I think best of his papers there.

'The mail is closing: I have not said a tithe of what is in my mind, and I must hurry. Although it is certain that Acland hated his wife, and wished to do her as much injury as possible by making such a will, yet if she was what he declares, and if her children have the estates, why, then, the loss of this money will not ruin her. Perhaps that should not be a final argument against my acceptance of it with honour. I did save his life, however, and I tried my best to save it again. The gift is not unearned, in a sense. And think what a difference it will make, not so much to me as to my mother and Grace! At the beginning of this letter I was almost desperate for want of pence, and within a few days a prospect of riches, enormous to me, has opened. I will not give it up without full inquiry.

'Perhaps Mrs. Acland is dead, and her daughter also, possibly. In that case I have no hesitation. The son is provided for. But I am running on in ignorance. Upon you, Vane, I rely to collect the information which must guide me. I know you would do so much for friendship, but I beg you to regard it as a matter of business. If it is not exactly etiquette for a barrister to undertake such inquiries, put them into the hands of a confidential lawyer. And meanwhile address your first impressions to Meerut, where we shall be established before a reply could reach me. And pray, my dear Vane, recollect what my anxiety will be until you can forward a definite opinion.

'Yours ever,

'RICHARD SAXELL.

'Rupert Vane, Paper Buildings, Temple.

'P.S.—For heaven's sake, not a word to my mother! I beg you to regard this as an imperative condition.'

'Meerut, Jan. 17.

'DEAR VANE,

'I have forwarded to you to-day every scrap of paper found in Raikes's quarters here. They show, as we thought, that this assumption of his identity with Hugh Acland was no deathbed fancy. A lawyer's trained intelligence may observe many points that escape me. You will find, however, allusions of very long date, and many broken imprecations on his wife, such as he repeated to us. The diaries are much mutilated, and I suppose a court of law might hesitate to admit them in such form. Yet the facts positive are there, and the pages torn out may have referred to quite other matters, which Acland did not care to preserve when ordered on campaign. St. Paul has seen everything. I almost wish he had not now, but of that presently. He sealed them up in due form.

'The story suggested by these fragments seems plain enough, and it is what I told you, with more detail. Acland fell in love with a beautiful girl at Oxford, beneath him in station; deceived her apparently, but married her a few weeks before a son was born. His father cut him off, and the pair were as miserable as he at least deserved to be. Connected somehow with the betrayal was Julius Beaver, evidently a rich man, and evidently feared as well as hated by Acland. The latter seems to have discovered—or, I should say, he vehemently suspected—that Beaver and his wife were playing him false a few years after the marriage. The evidence is not stated, but Acland's jealousy and rage are shown in a score of violent passages. He assaulted Beaver desperately, ingeniously made it appear that he was drowned, and vanished for ever. There the case is, in brief.

'I know you will look into it for me. The first step is to ascertain the mere facts—whether the uncle is alive, or the father, or Mrs. Acland, or her children? Then you will learn easily enough whether there was any money, and what has become of it. You quite understand my position, I trust. If I can lay claim to this bequest, honestly and honourably, I will pursue it; by honestly I mean that Raikes or Acland had it justly to leave, and by honourably I mean that no innocent person will be gravely affected by the loss of it. On these conditions, you will shape your course resolutely.

'There is a simple step I recommend as a soldier, subject to your discretion. You may send your clerk to the Adjutant-General's office; let him find the date of John Raikes's enlistment—it was at Westminster, December 14, 1862—and take down the names of every recruit who joined within a short time of that day. It will be easy to trace them; and let him hunt up those who joined the Artillery. Recruits feel rather lost in barracks; they fraternize and gossip. Although I don't suppose that Acland was a man to tell his secrets, he must have been particularly lonely, and there is the chance. He evidently drank, and under such circumstances he would probably drink harder. If you find among the Artillery recruits any described as "well-educated," direct special attention to them. They would be Acland's friends, if they came within his reach.

'That is all I have to say on the direct issue, but you will allow me to mention something, not for yourself, but in view of the probability that you may have to employ a lawyer, or to show papers to an agent of the other party—if there be one. The circumstances and conditions of Acland's marriage cannot affect my interests, so far as I see; if they did, if I am bound to go into all that, the persons affected being alive, I would almost throw the matter up this instant. But I do not see how they can be brought into any questions that may arise. The vague accusations of his wife's misconduct with Beaver cannot be suppressed altogether, I fear, since they are contained in the diaries all through; but the other matter is only named in a rambling manuscript, which seems to have been intended for a declaration of Acland's wrongs and grievances against his wife. They have nothing to do with me. If he behaved to her like a scoundrel in the beginning, and if she avenged herself afterwards, Acland was the only man who has no right to reproach her. I do not know that she did, and I have no wish to know. Therefore, keep that manuscript back. To tell the truth, Vane, I would not have sent it even to you, but St. Paul insisted.

'He has also compelled me to forward the rough draft of a letter dated three years since, from Mhow, and addressed to Miss Acland; so I understand the very fragmentary hints, but it is difficult to believe that a man could write a cold-blooded narrative of her mother's weakness and guilt to a young girl. That draft is the ugliest feature in an ugly tale. I vainly repeat to myself that it does not alter facts, that the legacy of a scoundrel, if honestly earned, is as valid as that of a saint. My only comfort is that the letter perhaps was never sent, or never received. I could almost hope that the girl had died before it reached her.

'Now I have done. You can guess my anxiety to hear from you.

'Yours ever, my clear Vane,

'RICHARD SAXELL.

'Rupert Vane, Paper Buildings, Temple.'

CHAPTER II.
SCARSHOLME.

THE holiday visitor has seldom a good word for Scarsholme. His experience mostly justifies an emphatic belief that it never stops raining there. But residents tell another story. They declare that the sentinels of the sky keep an anxious watch over that secluded glen. Always there is a scurrying of clouds aloft, now in balls and drifty battalions, now in big masses which surge above the hill-tops, and swell slowly into sight until the broad heaven is canopied. If strangers be spied approaching, these clouds pour a deluge; but when the village rests at peace, and no forms appear but those familiar, approved of heaven and men, they drop just so much moisture as the earth implores, and slide away. And when the sun shines at Scarsholme, no spot is more lovely. The hills around it gleam and sparkle, the still tarns glisten, the tiny 'forces' leap in ribbons of white foam from cliff to brae. Far-stretching pinewoods, blue in the distance, black-green at hand, fill every gap in the coronet of hills. Yellow pastures, hedged by walls of stone, chequer the bleak fell. Skeletons of mighty rocks lie half-hid among brambles, tall fern, golden gorse, and purple heather.

The Picts' Scaur is a conspicuous landmark. Every dalesman not a downright infidel believes that this grey shoot was channelled by invading savages, who slid down the hill sitting on their shields. A small cottage stands at the foot of Picts' Scaur in its own pretty grounds, divided from the road by a little brook. All about the place shows refinement and ease. The bridge is graceful; the stream-banks are planted with taste. From the drawing-room of the cottage opens a conservatory, of that handsome size which demands a stove and a good gardener. Such a dainty little house it is that one naturally looks for the stable, and one finds it charmingly concealed beside the vinery. Quite a little picture, thinks the tourist, surveying it with rueful admiration, as he recalls his dull villa at Bradford or Birmingham. People who live there must needs be happy he thinks, and he asks their name. The coachman replies that all this country belongs to Lord Rainforth, of Daneham Castle. His tenant in the cottage, who has made great improvements, is Mrs. Saxell, a widow lady, whose son distinguished himself so much in Afghanistan during the war. The coachman seldom fails to add that her niece, Miss Palliser, is the handsomest young lady of those parts. And all the tourist party agree that Mrs. Saxell must be a happy woman.

But she does not look happy at all on a bright June day, poring over household books and papers. Handsomely and fashionably she is dressed in a quiet way; everything in the room is handsome and fashionable in a quiet way. The furniture is not new; some of it, in fact, is a good deal worn, but it bears evidence of taste and costliness. Even the cat, dozing at the sunny window, is thorough-bred Persian.

The lady's face is naturally harsh of outline and austere, with large black eyes, full of questioning and suspicion—the face of one obstinate but flighty, quick to imagine evil, fierce to resent it, but not ill-tempered nor unamiable while things go smoothly. Things are not going smoothly to-day, however, and Mrs. Saxell's frown becomes more and more grim as she reads and notes. The budget is embarrassed.

A bright young creature enters, tall and lithe, in that sweetest age of girlhood which, for a figure like hers, promises a stately fulness. The face is absolutely beautiful, fair, blue-eyed, rosy, without a fault. That is, no doubt, the supremest type of loveliness, regarded as a mere development of colour and shape. Every man sees its perfection, and perhaps the dullest clown is not less affected thereby than is the keenest judge of beauty. But the latter may not be attracted beyond eye-worship, for such charms, however exquisite, are apt to be co-related to a weak and commonplace character.

The rule did not apply in this case: Miss Palliser did not look feeble in any sense, and certainly not uninteresting. A wilful and impulsive spirit dwelt in her lovely eyes; the laughing mouth showed both firmness and daring. It was not a clever face, nor perhaps very amiable; but quick and good-tempered.

'You sent for me, auntie?' she said.

The gaze of Medusa could have been hardly more severe than that which this young person met so gaily.

'I demand,' said Mrs. Saxell,' an explanation of this item in Armside's bill. He charges you with twenty yards of real Dacca muslin, at five shillings a yard, and five yards of silk at eight and sixpence. What does it mean?'

'Oh, don't look at me over your spectacles, auntie! You look like Minerva and her owl at once!'

'I insist on a serious answer. What is the meaning of this charge which is put down to last week?'

'Why, the meaning of it is a dress for Lord Rainforth's ball. Chumpy Armstrong is coming in to-day to make it. Isn't that economical?'

'You have dresses enough. I shall return all this unnecessary material!'

'Armside won't take Indian muslin back. He got it expressly for me. Make the best of it, auntie dear, and you'll see how nice I shall look.'

'Such thoughtlessness is wicked, Grace. Armside's bill comes to £46 3s. 6d., and where am I to find the money? My poor Richard! This is how a silly girl wastes the money you earn at the risk of your life!'

A preliminary pout, delicious to observe, but threatening. 'Don't brine: in Dick, please, auntie. He would not object to my spending a very few pounds for a ball at Daneham.'

'He would object, if he were wise, to your going at all. "When girls are engaged they ought not to go to balls—that's my opinion.'

'It isn't Dick's, nor mine. And if engaged girls should not go out, it's much more unbecoming for married women;—but you didn't shut yourself up, auntie. As for the dress, I could have got on very well without a new rosary. Take it out of my allowance.'

'Your allowance was forestalled last quarter. It is not calculated on a scale to buy Indian muslins.'

'Nor to build rosaries!' Grace said to herself.

'What did you mutter? Are you incapable of perceiving what must be the end of all this extravagance? Ruin stares us in the face!'

'Well, auntie, really now, is it my fault? Girls must have dresses, but they want very little else. May I go?'

'It was thoughtless of me to summon you from your silly occupations.'

Grace went out, with an impatient pursing of the lips. But she turned, and saw her aunt miserably bent over the figures. Swift and graceful she sped back, and kissed the faded cheek impetuously, crying:

'Don't trouble about those wretched bills, dear. You can say Dick is coming home, and then all will be right.'

'Don't speak of Richard, Grace! It is terrible for a mother when she dreads to think of meeting her son. There! You are going to the Rectory! Be home to lunch. And by-the-bye, as you pass Foote's shop, tell him his men went away at five o'clock last night. It's shameful, when the days are so long. They might have finished the rosary a week since, but they wish to increase their bill, the unprincipled artisans! Tell Foote this downright.'

'I will, in so many words.'

Grace bounded out, and Mrs. Saxell indulged a short but comforting reverie on the delights expected from her new rose-house. Then, with redoubled sternness, she set herself to studying a hopeless budget. This duty was not often performed. So long as her balance at the little Scarsholme Bank was not absolutely ridiculous, bills accumulated unread. But when the courteous manager reluctantly called attention to the fact that she was overdrawing, Mrs. Saxell became very flurried. This was an occasion of peculiar anxiety. By the last mail, her son spoke with some confidence of returning home; his mother speculated in alarm whether he was counting upon her economies to tide them over the furlough.

For an hour, with intervals of bewildered retrospect, Mrs. Saxell examined her situation; at the end of that time, a sound of wheels drew her, not reluctant, to the window. A dogcart familiar to all the inhabitants of Scarsholme as belonging to the Station Hotel, at Preston, passed up the little drive. By the coachman sat a tall young man in tweeds and pot-hat. Mrs. Maxell recognised a tourist. A little waterfall in the grounds sometimes attracted that variety of the human race, and her servants were used to deal with them. She went back to the accounts.

Presently entered a maid, 'If you please, 'm, the gentleman wants to see you,' and handed a card.

'Mr. Hugh Acland? Tell him I am very sorry, but I can make no exceptions. The waterfall is strictly private.'

The maid returned. 'Please, 'm, he insists on seeing you. He asked particularly if you read the name on his card.'

'Say I did, and that it conveyed no reason why the rule should be violated in his case.'

Re-entry of maid. 'Please, 'm, he swore at the waterfall, and he says——Oh, 'm, here he is!'

The visitor brushed past, and stood before Mrs. Saxell, a youth with sharp but handsome features and quick eyes.

'Let me correct this young person' he said. 'I did not swear at the waterfall, but expressed a hasty wish that it might be suppressed by—in fact, a dam. May I have the honour of a few minutes' conversation with you alone, madam?'

'I am sorry you should be disappointed, sir, but really the waterfall is not worth the praises that have been bestowed upon it, and——'

'Excuse me, Mrs. Saxell—I have the honour to address Mrs. Saxell? Then I must ask, did you really glance at my card? And it conveyed to you the idea that I was looking for bits of scenery?'

'It conveyed to me no idea at all, sir.'

'This is most extraordinary! My name is Acland, madam.'

Mrs. Saxell reviewed in spirit all the headings of her bills, found no Acland there, and answered sternly, 'Well, sir?'

'It is stupendous! A call from Hugh Acland does not surprise you?'

'It surprises me only in the sense that I cannot account for it.'

'Well, then, madam, let me tell you, since you forget the name, that I am the man, and the brother of the young lady, against whose fortune your son has made some cock-and-bull claim.'

'If you are not mad, sir, I can only reply that whatever my son does is certainly right and just.' She rang.

'Do I understand that you are not advised of Captain Saxell's pretensions? That shows, I think, what they are worth. "When a man keeps a secret from his mother he cannot have much confidence in his story. I must explain, then.'

'If you think proper, sir.'

The maid entered. 'Call the gardener,' Mrs. Saxell said, 'and any man about the place. Keep them in the kitchen till wanted. I shall be glad to hear your explanation, sir.'

'I have first to beg pardon, since you are unacquainted——'

'Never mind that! The facts!'

'The facts come to this. My father was drowned nearly twenty years ago. A scoundrel who belonged to Captain Saxell's battery, mortally wounded in the affair of the Guaja Pass last November, made a will under my father's name, in which he left the personal property my father would have in herited, which is now in possession of my mother, my sister, and myself, to your son——'

'Allow me! How could this man will away your father's property?'

'He declared, I say, that he was my father, not drowned, as all the world knew he was. The villain's story went that he resolved to disappear, and for this purpose made people believe him drowned, whilst he enlisted in the Artillery. And on his deathbed he pretended to confess.'

I shall not try to sketch the effect of the communication on Mrs. Saxell. But if she could not quite control her features she remained mistress of her nerves.

'I am obliged to you for telling me all this. But now, may I ask your motive in calling?'

'It seemed to me probable, madam, that your son, a distinguished soldier, may have been deceived by a plausible scoundrel——'

'Who was dying?'

'That seems a most important point until you have heard my explanation. I have come here now, madam, against the advice of everyone, even of your son's friend, Mr. Vane. I said to myself, men are selfish and contemptible creatures, willing to risk their souls for money——'

'Referring that profound observation of experience to my son?'

The youth was so utterly confounded that he could not speak for a moment.

Grimly satisfied, Mrs. Saxell resumed:

'Proceed, I beg; you did not refer the observations to my son in particular.'

'No!' he eagerly exclaimed. 'I assure you I did not! And I do not know by experience that men will sell their souls. Pray forget that silly remark.'

'Is it worth while to go further? The matter seems to come to this: You wish me to interfere in this action. I know no more of it than you have told. But if my son claims what you say is your property, on legal grounds, the question for me lies between your word and his. Judge which a mother takes!'

'But allow me to explain. We know very well who Sergeant-Major Raikes was, and we can prove it to the satisfaction of honest people——'

'My son's legal adviser is an honest person, I don't doubt. You had better explain to him.'

She rang the bell, and Mary entered with a curious promptitude. 'Show this gentleman out.'

'But will you not listen, madam? I wish to avoid a painful and expensive in-quiry by——'

'Insulting a mother, not once, but again and again. Send the men in, Mary!'

'Indeed I did not mean to insult you. Taking it for granted that Captain Saxell's mother knew all, I naturally thought she would understand my position. I apolo-gize, madam!'

'There is still time to go with dignity.'

Two brawny North-countrymen appeared at the door, amusement gleaming in their light, shrewd eyes. Acland stood quite unembarrassed, looking at Mrs. Saxell.

'Show this young man to his vehicle/ she said loftily.

'Oh, I cannot object, if it's put in that way! But a guard of honour walks first, I believe. Right about face, men! quick march!'

They grinned, waiting for orders. Mrs. Saxell coloured with anger.

'I command you to leave my house, sir!'

'Indeed, I do not wish to offend you. If these good fellows will walk first, I'll follow like a——'

He stopped short. Grace was standing in the doorway, wide-eyed, between the two rustics.

'And if not?'

'If not——then I will all the same, renewing my apologies for the intrusion.'

He bowed, his eyes fixed on Grace, and went. A moment afterwards the dog-cart drove away. As it passed the window, Acland looked in and raised his hat.

'What *is* the matter? "Who is that young man?'

'A very vulgar and impertinent boy, who called on business. I must consult a lawyer, and where to find one honest and capable in this neighbourhood I don't know. There's Mr. Vane. Why, he mentioned Mr. Vane, my son's friend! How ter-ribly confusing it is!'

'Then tell me, aunt!'

'It is nothing to interest you!'

The pretty face clouded.

'I won't be put off in this silly way, aunt!'

'Grace! Recollect yourself!'

'I recollect that I am eighteen years old, engaged to marry Dick, who is, somehow, concerned in this matter; and therefore I have a right to know what it is.'

'When I was young, ladies did not speak of their engagements in this tone.'

'But you always say that they were companions and comforts to their parents, whilst we are selfish triflers. Let me play one character or the other—or rather let me combine the two.'

Mrs. Saxell, in truth, felt the need of an adviser. Her firmness was not generally supported by intelligent strength of mind. When a resolution was taken she clung to it pitilessly, as much, perhaps, because she distrusted her own judgment in changing, as because she was satisfied to pursue the former course. Grace knew her disposition thoroughly, and played on it with confidence.

So at length the bewildering story was told, Grace listening in amazement, her eyes open to their utmost width, her beautiful lips parted. But the young lady had a clear brain and presence of mind imperturbable. She saw daylight through the confusion, and exclaimed, when the tale was finished:

'Now, auntie, write a telegram at once, and I will take it.'

'A telegram? It's a shilling a word, I believe.'

'No, no! Not to Dick! To Mr. Vane!'

'You display my folly in trusting a child "with secrets who instantly repeats them to all the world.'

'You forget, dear! Mr. Vane knows all about the matter, evidently. Besides, you need not commit yourself in a telegram, even if there were a secret about it.'

'It is never prudent to talk in business. Act!'

'But if you don't ask Mr. Vane, how will you discover what it all means?'

The argument struck Mrs. Saxell. She said presently:

'I never sent a telegram in my life.'

This with the air of a virtuous person urged to commit forgery.

'Nor I. It will be delightful. Write at once, auntie!'

Mrs. Saxell frowned, reflected, arranged her paper, and frowned again. After interrogating the walls with silent severity, she observed:

'I do not see how to put it with the delicacy required.'

'Let me, dear! "Mrs. Saxell, Scarsholme, to Rupert Vane, Esq., Paper Buildings, Temple. Mr. Hugh Acland has been here"—cross out "been," say "called"—"speaks of claim my son makes on him——" '

'Why, Grace, all the village will know about it!'

'Of course! that won't do. Write "speaks of claim made against him. Is it true claim made?" Sixteen words. Add "Reply immediately. We anxious." There! If Mr. Vane knows about the matter, he will understand. We should get a reply to-night. Oh, how long the afternoon will be! Now, I will take it to the office before lunch.'

'My dear, a young lady cannot be entrusted with a telegraphic message of this importance. I will carry it myself.'

'Oh, bother—I mean, do pray make haste, dear auntie! I will bring your bonnet'

'No, no. I cannot be flustered thus.'

'Remember, if we are not quick we shall not get the answer to-night. Let me go with you, at least.'

Under this stimulus, aided by Grace's deft hands, Mrs. Saxell was not so long as usual in preparing, and they set forth. There was a sternness in the old lady's carriage, and a concentrated rigidity in her eye when she walked abroad, which daunted even that independent race of men who dwell at Scarsholme; but upon this occasion her solemnity was awful. She entered the telegraph office with the air of an executioner who is determined not to heed the entreaties of his victim, and spoke to the mild young person established there in tones that thrilled her with an overpowering sense of her responsibilities toward the State. More impressive still, if possible, was Mrs. Saxell's demeanour in returning from this expedition. Grace felt inclined to shake her aunt and run away.

That afternoon was longer than even Grace expected, but at dinner-time the answer came. Mrs. Saxell received it with a trembling hand, and glowered speechlessly at the servant, too nervous to read. Grace snatched and tore it open:

' "True such claim made. Have taken necessary steps. I kept it secret at Richard's express desire. Will write." Dick wished to spare us disappointment, the dear fellow! But Mr. Acland is evidently alarmed, and that is a good sign. Auntie dear, we can't rest in this uncertainty. We must go to town to-morrow.'

'Your society would be a great comfort, but I do not see what useful purpose——'

'Why, ungrateful relative, who suggested the telegram that obtained you this delightfully exciting reply? In London you will be——' lost, Grace was about to say, but she prudently substituted 'dull, with no one to speak to.'

'That is very true. But I should probably stay only two nights. And we have the expense to consider.'

'It is not worth while to grudge a few pounds when Ave are going to talk of thousands.'

'Thousands?' repeated Mrs. Saxell, catching her breath in a kind of snort, 'Thousands?'

'Did you think it was a hundred or two? You dear old innocent auntie!'

'I have not considered it. Why do you say thousands?'

'Ever so many reasons. In the first place, Dick kept the matter a secret. He would not have done that if it had been a trifle.'

'He did very wrong, whether it was a trifle or not. A man has no adviser so sound and so disinterested as his mother. I am very much grieved, and even indignant, at Richard's conduct.'

'The single thing we can be sure of is that he thought he was acting for the best. However, you admit he would not have left us ignorant if it had been a small affair. Then, Mr. Acland would not have taken the trouble to come down. The address on his card is Eaton Square. That's a very rich neighbourhood, isn't it?'

'So I am informed. There is something in that, too.'

'One could see that he is a man of position,'

'I saw that he was very rude and unmannerly. A foolish young man. too.'

'Yes, dear, but not vulgar; and awfully conceited, but not snobbish. I conclude from his visit, his evident anxiety, and Dick's silence, that the question is important. What do men think important in affairs of money? Not a bill like Arm-side's for forty pounds something! Therefore, I conclude that one may safely talk of thousands in this matter.'

'I do not encourage you,' said Mrs. Saxell, with patronizing complacency, 'to give your imagination play upon general subjects. But in this case it may have led you towards the truth. I wonder what the sum will prove to be!'

'Putting one thing with another, I should say not less than fifty thousand—perhaps more.'

'Fifty thousand pounds? But, any dear! Recollect that this sum was left by a man who occupied the honourable but subordinate post of sergeant-major in Richard's battery. If he could have claimed one-fiftieth of that, is it credible that he would not have done so?'

'That argument goes too far, dear. If he could have claimed a thousand or a hundred or a five-pound note without some inconvenience, would he not have done so? The figure even may have alarmed him. We must suppose that Mr. Acland did not choose to return to life. He may have committed a crime, you know. Anyway, his indifference or neglect, or whatever the feeling may have been, proves nothing as to the amount, since we have agreed that young Mr. Acland would not be likely to trouble himself about a few hundreds. I go in for fifty thousand at least.'

'Oh, how happy we shall be, Grace, if it's half of that!' cried Mrs. Saxell. Recollecting herself, she added sternly, 'But I do not allow your childish imagination to run away with me. To think, as an exercise of fancy, what good deeds might be performed with such a sum gives a pleasing exhilaration. That is all.'

'Dear Dick would come home at once. I don't think I should wish him to leave the Service, aunt. A civilian is poor with fifty thousand pounds; but a gallant soldier, distinguished and decorated, may look down upon a duke. The fortune will give us confidence, you know.'

This little speech reminded Mrs. Saxell that the money, whatever it might be, was not offered to her, but to her son and this chit, his promised wife. Forthwith she remembered her grievance.

'Richard acted for the best as he thought, no doubt; but he should not have kept a matter of such importance from his mother. It was not dutiful.'

'Oh, aunt, Dick is the best of sons!'

'He is a good son, but weak, I fear, in some respects. It is most fortunate that the imprudence of that silly young man has given me warning. He himself possibly is not of a designing nature, but his friends evidently are. Richard would be easily talked over in a money matter, and I esteem Mr. Vane rather as an obliging friend than as a sound man of business.'

'He's very clever, isn't he?'

'I believe so, in his papers and lawbooks. But not to be trusted with great interests among unscrupulous persons.'

'Your imagination has gone far beyond me, aunt. Mr. Acland does not look unscrupulous.'

'And remark that he is not trusted by the elders! Moreover, appearances are deceptive, especially with the young-. He came here to explain something, as I understood, which "honest people" would believe, the effect of which would be to suppress Richard's claim.'

When Mrs. Saxell emerged from 'facts,' which, bewildered her, into the realm of abstract suspicion, she was clear and pointed enough.

' " Honest people," ' she continued, c is generally a polite term for fools, since fools is the plain English description for people who allow themselves to be talked over. Depend upon it that in an action of this kind there are always underhand proceedings, more or less reprehensible. It is prudent to suspect everybody in such a case, and every word; but above all to suspect explanations. If Richard is not to be defrauded I must take his interests in hand. It is very strange he should have wished to keep me out, of it, but stranger to those who disbelieve in the beneficent ways of Providence that an accident, as they would profanely call it, should have disconcerted his silly plans. I shall now insist on receiving my son's full confidence through Mr. Vane.'

Grace looked at her aunt curiously. She was not used to think the lady very wise, but perhaps, she said to herself, Dick might have a less judicious counsellor in this case. No fear that his interests would suffer through Mrs. Saxell's want of attention; nor that they would be surrendered through weakness or pity. Her spirit was like Catiline's and that of many spendthrifts—careless of money belonging to herself, incapable of forethought in everyday affairs, but keen and active and determined in pursuing a chance of gain.

The conference broke up under a sudden anxiety of both ladies to be 'packed' in time. Mrs. Saxell took only one portmanteau, but to arrange it was a toilsome operation. She reflected, made up her mind severely upon grounds of pure reason, and gave hurried orders. But there was a lack of *ensemble* in her strategy. The introduction of each separate object necessitated a re-arrangement of everything disposed before. The General had no concerted plan, and when a dress deployed, as it were, or a hairbrush sought to take the order which exact tactics approved, some other body always stood in the way.

Grace pursued the opposite system. She packed the portmanteau, a bag and a luncheon-basket as fast as she could stow them. Then she went to bed, and remembered a score of things actually essential. It was not worth while to rise—in the morning there would be time enough; but in the morning she could remember none of them. Mrs. Saxell had given herself and all about her vast trouble overnight; but when the moment of action came she was ready. Poor Grace was flurried and scurried, laughing and half crying; and she started at length without several necessaries, whilst her trunk was full of useless things. They caught the train, however; and what trouble is worth reckoning by a girl on her first visit to London!

CHAPTER III.
LORD DUNSCOMBE.

VERY mixed were the reflections of Mr. Hugh Acland as he drove back in haste to catch the afternoon express; but I need not dwell upon them. By half-past eight o'clock he was at home in Eaton Square, dressed for dinner, and he found the ladies waiting.

'Good-evening, mams. Good-evening, Edie. Anyone coming to-night?'

'Only Lord Dunscombe,' said Mrs. Acland. 'Mr. Vane's name was on your memoranda, but crossed out.'

'Yes, I distrust Vane. A man can't be the disinterested friend of both parties in a case like ours. I wrote and told him so; and he probably sees the truth of my remark, since he has not answered.'

'More hasty work for your mother to undo!'

'Is it necessary to keep friends with Vane! Well, you have all the diplomatic talent of the family, mams, and my business is to find it employment. What have you been about all day, little sister?'

'The usual thing. A girl's time is so stupid that it's cruel to ask an account. What have you been doing, Hughie? We haven't had a glimpse of you since yesterday afternoon.'

'I'll tell you one thing I've been, done or suffered. I've seen the loveliest girl in the universe!'

'Dear me! This before Edie?'

'Oh, I do our princess so much justice that I believe only her brother could think Grace the loveliest creature in the world. Others would stand awe-struck and bewildered between the two.'

'Like the ass we read of! Never mind me! Who is Grace?'

'Yes, who is Grace? Lord Dunscombe, who is Grace?'

The new-comer was a very handsome man, tall, fair-haired, with the complexion of a girl, bronzed, not burnt, by Indian suns. His large eyes were grave and quiet, but the full red mouth and the crease between his smooth brows betrayed passion and temper.

'Grace?' he repeated thoughtfully.

'Oh, Dunscombe is going to review all the Graces in the universe, and to answer your conundrum in a twelvemonth—wrong. I'll tell you who she is—Grace Palliser, the niece of Mrs. Saxell.'

'Mrs. Saxell!' exclaimed both the ladies; but dinner was announced at this moment.

Edie sat grave and silent through the meal, but that was her usual habit. Nothing' was said about Grace before the servants, but when they had withdrawn, she exclaimed abruptly:

'How did you come to see Mrs. Saxell's niece, Hugh? Are they in town?'

'They are at Scarsholme, a charming place. By-the-bye, Dunscombe, it mostly belongs to your father. I congratulate you.'

'I thought the name of Saxell was familiar, somehow. So that is the lady? I have heard of the lovely Grace, then. I have even seen her, years ago'

'And what were you doing at Scarsholme, Hugh? Do you mean that you called on those people? What for? By whose advice? How incredibly foolish!'

Mrs. Acland interrupted.

'My dear child, these family explanations cannot interest Lord Dunscombe.'

'No; but Lord Dunscombe will be pleased to hear the latest news. "Well, Hugh?'

'Well, my little sister, I went to Scarsholme of my own accord. Would you believe it, mams, Mrs. Saxell knew nothing of the business?'

'No, I would not believe it!' Edie said decisively.

'It's true, nevertheless. She could not have deceived me.'

Edie made an impatient gesture.

'And what passed?' said Mrs. Acland.

'The old dragon would not talk things over quietly. If Captain Saxell takes after his mother, we may gird up our loins for a real fight. She is as grim and as angular as the queen of clubs. Our interview ended with a situation. The old lady fetched two cads to pitch me out of doors, and I don't know what would have happened had not Grace made her appearance.'

'You seem to have got on intimate terms with the young lady in a short time!'

'Then I went away. We didn't even peak. The driver told me who she was.'

'But what did you say? How did you explain your visit?' cried Edie.

'Mrs. Saxell would hear no explanation. With that respect for the head of a family which my little sister does not emulate, she rowed that whatever her son did was right, and called her myrmidons to expel the blasphemer.'

'What will people say of this, Lord Dunscombe? How will it affect the betting on our case? The clubs will hardly accept the ingenuous story as it stands. It's a round maxim in life, I have been told, never to give credit to an adversary for downright madness.'

Hugh flushed.

'My dear Edie,' Mrs. Acland interrupted in her pleasant way, 'you allow your feelings to affect your temper, which is unladylike. These little tiffs are not common in my family, Lord Dunscombe.'

'You have honoured me with so many opportunities to judge that I could not be misled on that point. Depend on it, Miss Acland, the club will never learn of Hugh's escapade from me.'

'Oh,' said she carelessly, rising, 'I did not suspect you of tattling. Here's a kiss of forgiveness, my silly little brother.'

The two men kept silence for a time. Hugh said at length:

'The mams allows us to smoke here.'

They lit. Another pause.

'By-the-bye, Dunscombe, are people talking much about this disagreeable business of ours? You know all that goes on.'

'Frankly, they are talking, of course. After that paragraph in the *Age,* everybody is asking everybody what it means; but no one can answer exactly. I suppose I am better informed than most, thanks to Mrs. Acland's confidence—which I value very highly, Hugh, I assure you—but I know hardly anything.'

'I wish the dear old mams would extend more of her confidence to me, for I'm almost as ignorant. Doesn't it strike you its absurd that I should be kept out of the secret in this way?—I don't mean the secret, but out of the details, you know. As my father's son I have a sentimental interest that seems worth attention, and as his heir I am the principal party concerned.'

'I thought the will did not touch your landed property?'

'Of course not; but if it were anything but an act of spiteful madness or an hallucination, it would take the most of my cash, deprive my mother of her income and my sister of her fortune, and that would come to much the same thing for me. Don't you think it's monstrous——'

Hugh stopped suddenly, flashing. He was impetuous and frank of speech, not to say thoughtless, and it only occurred to his mind at that instant that he was complaining of his mother.

Dunscombe answered the idea, not heeding the interruption.

'So you went to assert yourself with Mrs. Saxell? Do you think that, on the whole, you made anything of that?'

'I must confess that I didn't, so far,' Hugh answered unwillingly.

'Speaking for myself,' Dunscombe continued, 'without any reference to matters where I can't follow you, I will say that my respect and admiration of Mrs. Acland is such that, if I held an opinion opposed to hers, I should think many times before I acted on it.'

Hugh looked at him sharply, as if feeling the point of the lesson and resenting it.

Dunscombe added hastily:

'Pray don't imagine that I am advising you. My remarks are quite in the abstract.'

'So I should suppose, of course,' Hugh said drily. 'But perhaps that visit to Scarsholme was injudicious.'

'Mrs. Acland does not seem much concerned.'

'Oh, she never does! But Edie's feeling about those people is downright savage. You know, Dunscombe, I can't honestly blame Saxell—not in my heart of hearts. He's a poor man, and it must be an awful temptation.'

'Ladies can't draw these distinctions.'

'I don't care,' Hugh continued. 'To see that beautiful creature would justify any imprudence. You never beheld a girl in a picture so lovely.'

'Indeed!'

'You are thinking of Edie—eh? By-the-bye, have you reflected that you have no small interest in our family trouble? That is, if you are still of the same mind.'

'Captain Saxell lays no claim to Miss Acland's hand, I believe.'

'You are not mercenary, anyhow.'

A pause.

'She does not care a pin for me, Hugh!' Dunscombe burst out.

'Well, my dear fellow, you know my sentiments. I like you immensely, but rather as a friend than as a brother-in-law. And look here, Dunscombe: as you have introduced the subject, I must say that I don't understand how you can speak seriously of marriage, leading the life you do.'

'I have never dared to speak of it, as you know. If I had the vaguest hope, I would live in a manner worthy of Miss Acland.'

'I hope so, for all our sakes. They say you find very pretty consolations meanwhile. But it's no business of mine.'

'I wish you would make it your business, Hugh. You don't doubt that I speak the truth?'

'Frankly, Dunscombe, I don't doubt that; but, as I told you long ago, I will not try to influence my sister either one way or the other. You are not the husband I should choose for her; but she is a girl who will choose for herself, and I grant you it's quite possible that the man she falls in love with will be very much less sympathetic to me than you are, though on other grounds, perhaps. Let us change the subject.'

'One moment, Hugh. I have sometimes feared—and I could not say what pain it has caused me—that Miss Acland may have made her choice already.'

'Otherwise she could not have resisted Lord Dunscombe? I can relieve you of that fear—Edie cares for no one.—Now, tell me, does Mrs. Saxell visit at Daneham?'

'Yes. Until my sister got engaged, she had a girlish admiration for your Grace. I often used to hear of her, and it's odd we have never met of late years.'

'Lucky for all parties, perhaps, excepting yourself.'

'And you, possibly. I shall have the pleasure soon, I dare say. My brother Ralph brings his bride home on the 27th, and the governor is inviting all the countryside to a ball. He makes a ridiculous fuss over Ralph.'

'You're not a loving brother, Dunscombe. I note that among other demerits that might have been personally interesting under other circumstances.'

'My dear fellow,' said Dunscombe anxiously, 'don't judge on imperfect knowledge. I like Ralph very well; but Rain-forth has been nagging me about him ever since we were boys. It isn't as if he was very clever or very good. I'll give you the explanation, Hugh. If Ralph were the eldest, my father would prefer me.'

'I say, get me an invitation to your place on the 27th.'

'Come with me as my peculiar guest; my mother shall send you an invitation to the ball. We have some odd customs in our family, which I will put you up to. There's the piano. Shall we go?'

Miss Acland played, as she did all else, correctly, brilliantly, without enthusiasm. "When Dunscombe asked what was the piece, she turned back to see. He expressed admiration of her skill in performing such difficult music at sight.

'Oh, I had practised it lots of times, without observing the composer's name. That isn't in the lesson.'

'You don't care for music, then?'

'Oh yes; it helps the clay along. There's dressing and breakfast and Ebony—that's my horse, you know—and dressing and lunch, and music and a drive, and dressing and tea, and dressing and dinner, and talk and bed.'

'No reading, Edie?' asked her mother.

'That's exceptional, like a ball.'

'What a little humbug you are, Edie!'

'Explain yourself, sagacious brother.'

'You want to pose as a female cynic, despising human pleasures. Don't believe her, Dunscombe. She's a small volcano of sentiment and devotion, and all that'

'People who live on volcanoes don't suspect the fire underneath, sometimes. So you may be right, though I can't imagine how you should know.'

'I recollect former eruptions.'

'I never had any beside measles, and that was not bad—was it, mamma?'

'Hugh refers to mental outbursts,' replied Mrs. Acland, laughing.

'Then he is unkind and inaccurate. All my nurses will declare that there never was a child who broke out less.'

'I spoke metaphorically. Until two or three years ago you——'

'Oh, I don't understand metaphor.'

She began playing quietly to herself.

'My daughter is a very matter-of-fact young person, now,' said Mrs. Acland to Lord Dunscombe. 'But Hugh is right in saying that we recollect her in quite another character.'

'I am a little humbug, then?' Edie cried, wheeling round upon the music-stool. 'This becomes a serious charge. What is the basis? My harmless statement apparently that music occupies its due place among the day's events, like eating, and exercise, and talking nonsense. But doesn't it? Do I sit down to play because I am seized with an irresistible impulse? am I possessed? Not at all! I play because that is the proper thing to do at a certain hour, and it gives me a certain pleasing sensation, like eating. Music under such conditions is the dullest and least poetic of all the customary events I named. When I sit down to dinner I don't know what is coming. When I ride, I can go which way I will, and perhaps I shall not return to the place I started from. When I talk, I don't know what I shall say or what the other person will answer. But when I open my music-box and my book, the process and the result are only a matter of chords and strings. There is not an atom of my own self in the sounds which an eminent composer has arranged for me, and an eminent manufacturer has supplied me with wires and bits of ivory to execute. The composer's soul may have found rest in it, but mine does not, except by a mere appropriation of his feelings. Mechanically I reproduce some one else's ideas on a machine, and that does not interest me more than any other conventionality.'

'But all music must be rendered by some instrument.' said Dunscombe.

'The voice is a machine, and our minds are machines. But there is such a thing as real music, nevertheless—a strain that tells its own story of passion or sadness, fresh from a human heart; the cry of a man or woman who could not keep silence under deep feeling, and spoke in tones that all the world will recognise for ever. That is music, as that is poetry. The day's events bring no such feeling to me.'

'I should like to hear real music,' said Dunscombe.

'Who would not?' she answered coolly.

'You have given a distinct challenge,' Mrs. Acland said, 'and, under the penalty of conviction for talking nonsense, you must illustrate the theory.'

'But, mamma, Lord Dunscombe does not understand! None of those composers wrote what was real music for me. I say that music is that which springs from the heart—the utterance of individual passion. I can copy or imitate, but reproduction is not real music. Besides, we must dress, mamma.'

'There is time. I think you ought to show what you mean, dear, if you mean anything.'

'Oh, it is so much trouble. And it excites me to repeat those screams of pathos! Do you insist?'

'My daughter, I command.'

'My sister, I imperatively implore!'

'That jars! I call this real music, Lord Dunscombe. Born, not manufactured.'

She struck a dozen wild notes, interrogative, sharply distinct, perilously near to discordance.

'The poet is hesitating what form to » give his thought,' said Edie, with conviction. 'Now he has it.'

A rush of sound, a clanging of human passions, through which ran a clear thread of melody, interrupted, pausing, struggling, but swelling at length to a burst of triumph, ceasing abruptly in a few dropped notes.

'What demoniac scream is that?' Hugh cried, his eyes aglow.

'They call it "Hunniades' March." Nobody made it. It grew! That's man's music—here is woman's.'

A sad, low theme, with changes and twists and returns to the original *motif,* broken by unexpected peals of laughter, which died into lingering sobs, and ended in slow despair.

'Where did you find such extraordinary compositions?' Mrs. Acland inquired wonderingly. 'They are mad!'

'Divinely mad, I think! That is called Roumanian, but it is old as human life and woman's suffering! Pray don't thank me, Lord Dunscombe. Good-night!'

Mrs. Acland said, 'You won't be late, Hugh? I must hare half an hour's conversation.'

'When my mother says "must," Dunscombe, we always obey; but she doesn't often test our virtue. Will one o'clock do, mams?'

'If you are punctual.'

'Count on me, dear! Good-night, dear little family humbug!'

'Hugh is a good boy,' his sister remarked when they had gone, 'but very silly!'

'That's tautology, my child! You said he was a boy! And he is—very!'

When Hugh returned, Mrs. Acland was waiting for him. 'To-morrow,' she said, 'you accompany me to Mr. Vane's chambers with our lawyer. You know the case in outline, but it is possible allusions may be made which will strike less painfully if I prepare you. Listen attentively, therefore, my son, for I need not say how distressing these reminiscences are to me.

'I have never concealed that my birth was not equal to your father's. My own father was an Independent minister at Oxford. An undergraduate at Christ Church paid me attentions, but I did not like him. This man, Hardwicke, introduced to me, as his friend, your father, who came up to the same college. We fell in love, but I dared not ask my parents to consent to our marriage, and Hugh was still more afraid. I made a terrible mistake, which has never ceased to bear its fruits: after a long resistance, I consented to a secret marriage. Hardwicke had long since pretended to be reconciled to his disappointment. He was now ordained, and he performed the marriage privately. I may mention here that doubts arose afterwards as to its legality, and we were married again.'

'Do I understand, mother,' cried Hugh hotly, 'that this point has been raised by Saxell?'

'Most certainly not! It has no interest for anyone, and I mention it only' because I wish to have no secrets from my son.

'By means we could not guess at the time, Hugh's father heard of the marriage, and withdrew his son's allowance; as for the uncle, whose fortune you inherit, he held no communication with either. I must tell you, Hugh, for the comprehension of my story, that all the Aclands were quarrelsome and jealous and vindictive.

'We should have been in difficulties at the outset, but my husband's mother died, leaving him a small fortune. He left the University and acknowledged me. We were neither wise nor prudent, and Hugh fell into bad hands. His greatest friend, besides Hardwicke, was a man named Beaver, whom they knew at Oxford, though he was considerably older than they.

'Beaver was our evil genius, and is—a man of enormous wealth, great talent, and unbearable selfishness and affectation. He professed to admire me—always in an impersonal manner, as if I had been a work of art.—It is painful for a mother to speak of these things to her son——'

'If an angel tried to misinterpret your conduct I should not believe him!'

'It is that knowledge which sustains me, my son! You will never doubt me, Hugh!'

'I know you too well, mother!'

They kissed fondly.

'I disliked and distrusted Beaver. But—I am laying bare all the truth to you!— he amused me, and he made life pleasant with endless schemes of diversion. I was innocent and thoughtless; your father, though passionate, was secret. He said afterwards that his jealousy had been aroused from the first, but I do not believe it. As soon as I learned the incredible truth I begged him to break off acquaintance with Beaver. But they had relations—of money I suppose—which forbade this. We remained in the same position, constantly associated with a man whom the husband suspected and the wife both hated and feared. A dreadful time. And it lasted" for months!'

'But, mother, is it possible my father was such a cur as to bear this state of things—for money?'

'I believe in my heart that he did not really doubt me. But his temper was reckless, the shifts he was put to had maddened him against all the world, and he avenged himself on me. Hugh was not a cur! He might have grown, under other circumstances, into a strong man. But, please do not interrupt—let me hurry on!

'Things became desperate with us. I do not know what projects Beaver and my husband had in view, but he suggested we should retire to Wolfingham, a village near his own home of Beaverlowe. This was in the autumn of 1862. Hardwicke had a curacy at Laystone, three miles away, and the three men were constantly together. At Wolfingham things grew worse and worse. One morning, after a terrible scene, Hugh rode away. I never saw him again, dead or alive.'

Mrs. Acland was deeply affected. Hugh took her hand and kissed her, murmuring consolation. What painful recollections had been lying under his mother's smiling face!

'He did not return that night, but I was not alarmed. The clergyman of the village came next morning with hints of calamity. I made him speak out. The horse your father was riding had regained the stable late, having evidently swum the river, which was in flood. There is a ford by Wolfingham Bridge, which Hugh was accustomed to use. Upon its farther bank they found hoof-marks where the horse had entered the water, but none to correspond on the near side. A hundred yards below the bridge, at a spot which was deep and dangerous at all times, they found prints, as though the horse had clambered out with difficulty. It had been swept beneath the bridge. Your father's hat was found some miles below, in a bush that overhung the stream.'

'This I have heard,' said Hugh, in a low voice.

'Captain Saxell's assertion is that your father was not drowned, but deliberately carried out a scheme to persuade us of his death. Wait! I am controlling myself, Hugh, to tell this story dispassionately; do not unnerve me! It is probable that Sergeant Raikes had not heard the evidence we possess; or he was too shrewd to raise questions by referring to it. According to his statement your father rode his horse half-way across the ford, dismounted, threw his hat into the stream, drove the horse into deep water, and returned. But there is an independent statement, that of a man named Peake, who was crossing Wolfingham Bridge at that hour. He told his story the next day, recollect. Peake heard cries in the river, and looking over the parapet he saw a body washed down. No one else was missing from the neighbourhood, and in all these years it has never been disputed that the body was your father's!'

'It was not found?'

'It was carried out to sea, no doubt.'

'And the inquiry proved nothing decisive?'

'There was no inquiry. Hugh's father returned my letters unopened, and his uncle did not answer them for months.'

'But when my great-uncle died?'

'That was six years afterwards. The trustees took it for granted, so far as I know, that Hugh was dead; if they made a serious inquiry I did not hear of it. You had twelve years of minority, and they may well have felt assured that if Hugh was still living he would 'certainly appear to claim his own in that time. Now, let me go back. This accident happened on December 9th, 1862—the evening of next day Edie was born. When I recovered full consciousness, I did not know where to turn for food.'

'My poor mother!'

'I hid myself in London, and lived by the sale of my jewellery. When that was exhausted, your great-uncle sought us out, and made an allowance. Now, give me all your attention. You know who Sergeant Raikes was?'

'His right name was Henry Hardwicke?'

'Yes, my husband's friend, and his bitter enemy! He also disappeared, two or three days later, under discreditable circumstances. It was on December 14th that Raikes enlisted in the Artillery at Westminster—not two days after Hugh's supposed death, as Captain Saxell declares in his case, since that occurred on the 9th, but two days probably after Hardwicke had vanished from Laystone. This man, Raikes, can be traced all through, of course, from the moment of his enlistment until he died, with a black lie in his mouth. He put his age at twenty-five years, the maximum for Artillery recruits, observe; Hugh had just reached that age, and he did not look it; but Hardwicke was twenty-eight. These details, however, and others more important I need not insist upon with you. Are there any questions that occur to your mind?'

'I must ask, mother, what part the man Leaver played at this time? Was he in the neighbourhood?'

'I believe he was, but we held no communication. Some hints reached me, mere gossip, of a fight between him and Hugh that evening, in which Beaver was badly hurt.

'Where did my father ride to?'

'Your father went to dine with Hardwicke, and he did. I see your drift, Hugh. But whatever may have been the truth in that scandal, Beaver had no part in Hugh's death. He was not the man to commit murder.'

'Did you see Peake?'

'I have never seen him. The clergyman of Wolfingham conducted what inquiries were made, and told me the result. My great object now is to find Peake, who certainly survives, and in a few days I hope to find him.'

'Where is he now?'

'We advertised, and the man answered, but lie is distrustful. A promise of reward, however, seems to be producing its effect, and we hope to see him shortly. Now, Hugh, you will be better able to follow the discussion to-morrow. It is not a formal meeting of lawyers.'

They parted tenderly.

Rupert Vane was a small, dried-up man, with the brows and eyes of a sage, the mouth of a sensitive woman. In matters that did not regard himself, when the result, if painful, would not come before his own eye, he rivalled Achitophel in the soundness, and if need be the cruelty, of his advice. But where his own interests or friendships were concerned, Vane showed hesitation and weakness. This seldom happened, of course, and he had already won standing as a junior of promise.

Mrs. Acland, Hugh, and their solicitor, Mr. Gorman, met at Vane's chambers next day.

'In suggesting this interview,' he said, 'I act upon the general drift of Captain Saxell's instructions. His anxious desire is to take no advantage, and he confidently hopes to be met in the same spirit. It is my good fortune that circumstances enable me to carry out this idea with special facilities. I have been acquainted with Mrs. Acland and esteemed her for many years, and Richard Saxell is my dearest friend. Knowing both parties so well, I have ventured to bring them face to face, as it were.

'Up to the present time I have not employed a solicitor. Captain Saxell does not profess to be indifferent about the issue. If he can claim this money with justice, and without inflicting a penalty too heavy on the present holders, he thinks he has earned it at the risk of his life, and he means to take it. As for the second of these conditions, if Mrs. Acland or her son take that ground, they will address themselves to the claimant direct. All I have to do at this first meeting is to hand over the papers with which I am furnished at present, and to explain Captain Saxell's position. Briefly, it is this: he acts absolutely on my discretion. If I find that the assertions of Sergeant Raikes are false, I am authorized to throw up the case. There can be no compromise. But unless they are proved to be so, Captain Saxell will proceed—as at present advised.'

'It is a responsible position for you,' said Mr. Gorman. 'In the event of your abandoning the Captain's claim, I understand that it passes to Mrs. Saxell?'

'Yes; but I opine that our refusal to persevere would seriously prejudice her chance. What I would urge, and I am sure of meeting the sympathy of Mrs. Acland and her son in the suggestion, is that they meet the facts advanced openly and straightforwardly. There is no reservation on Captain Saxell's part. All the evidence on which he relies has been laid in summary before Mr. Gorman, and I now offer copies of the originals. If new facts should arise, they will also be submitted. I add also a copy of the formal document by which Captain Saxell authorizes me to withdraw his claim instanter if I think right to take that course. It is to me a flattering proof of his friendship and confidence; to you an indisputable assurance of his sincere good faith. We work, therefore, not as enemies, but as rivals, anxious to discover the truth. The question before us, the whole question, practically is, Was Sergeant Raikes Hugh Acland, senior; or did that gentleman die, as was generally understood, in 1862?'

'Allow me,' said Hugh, 'there is another. If you can prove that Raikes was a man named Hardwicke, for instance, it would not be necessary to go further.'

'In that case he would not be Acland. Now, the first inquiry that arises is as to the handwriting. You have seen several specimens, Mrs. Acland, and here is a mass. I understand that though you do not declare the evidence of the handwriting conclusive to all the world, you are satisfied it is not your husband's?'

'It is the writing of a man who tries laboriously to imitate another person's hand. "Where Raikes scribbled hastily, as in notes which do not concern the case, his writing was utterly different to that of papers which have reference to it. Take these examples side by side.'

'It is very true, but most men have two handwritings at least,' said Vane.

'We hope to identify the scribbled hand, however,' said Gorman.

'I recognise it as that of Hardwicke,' Mrs. Acland declared. 'I am trying to obtain some acknowledged instances of his writing.'

'We think that Mr. Beaver, of Beaverlowe, has old letters of Hardwicke's. Probably that gentleman may be able to give valuable information, but he has not replied to Mrs. Acland as yet.'

'Well,' said Vane, J you have our case in every particular. We shall not press you in the least. May the right triumph, and I doubt not that it will.'

Hugh felt that he was squeezed out of the discussion in which he had so great an interest. Drawing aside, rather sullen, he turned over the papers and diaries laid out on a table.

'Many pages have been cut out here/ he cried suddenly. 'May I ask who cut them?'

Vane was silent, troubled; Gorman looked reproachfully at Mrs. Acland. Resolutely, but with heightened colour and eyes that burned, she met the inquiry. 'Those pages I have already seen, Hugh, and they were removed out of consideration for me and my son. Hardwicke was not a villain by halves! Now, Mr. Vane, allow us to express our gratitude for the very kindly and honourable manner in which you have presented this painful business. We beg you to convey the same assurance to Captain Saxell. He may depend on it we shall meet him with equal frankness.'

The clients withdrew; Gorman lingered. 'This is no common affair, Vane,' he said, 'and you are not treating it in a common manner. I confess I am more interested in it than in any case I recollect.'

'The one thing clear to me is that Raikes was a very extraordinary person. You did not know Hugh senior?'

'No; but from what I learn we could not rest our case upon the inherent improbability of his conduct,' Gorman replied. 'I mean, in pretending to be drowned, and serving twenty years in the ranks. He was wrong-headed enough for any eccentricity.'

'So I have heard. Mrs. Acland brought in all the good qualities the family can boast, they say. What an incredible villain Raikes must have been, whoever he was!'

'Mrs. Acland is her own lawyer, and I could take quite an unprejudiced view if there were anything to found a judgment on. One of the most extraordinary facts is that neither Acland nor Hardwicke seem to have had any friends in particular.'

'Not so extraordinary if Sergeant Raikes was a type of both! You forget Beaver.'

'Not likely! He was a worthy third, as far as I can gather.'

'I suspect that Beaver could tell us a good deal, if he liked.'

'So do I, but I suspect he won't if he can help it. We have made some inquiries about him. Whether it was the disgrace of the beating A eland gave him, or the shock of his death, or mere eccentricity that broke out at that time, we have no means of judging; but Beaver shut himself up from that day, and devoted his time to pictures and orchids.'

'That's not what I hear at all! He's a great hunting man, a model landlord, and all a country gentleman should be. So the}r say at the Rhadamanthus.'

'A good example of the old story. We are both right. But nobody sees him off the hunting-field, except his tenants. Beaverlowe used to be the liveliest house in the country; but never a guest has entered it these twenty years, nor has the master entered another house.'

'Mrs. Acland must have been very beautiful,' said Vane, with no apparent connection.

'And Beaver, they say, was very fascinating and very fast,' replied Gorman, laughing.

'Does that bear upon the case? I think we'd better drop the subject.'

'I am not at all sure that it does not bear upon the case, seeing that Acland was a mad brute. However, I don't ask your opinion.'

'I ask yours, then, without prejudice! Come, now!' said Vane.

'Upon ray honour, the more I think of it the more puzzled I am.'

CHAPTER IV.
IN HYDE PARK.

HUGH looked upon his mother as the dearest and best and cleverest of women. But this feeling did not reconcile him to the exclusion of his views and experience in the grave matter at issue. Young men of property learn self-confidence in affairs, if not wisdom, at an early age, and Hugh, perhaps, had more than his share. Beyond dispute, his interest in Captain Saxell's claim was most serious, both financial and sentimental, but he found himself put in the background. Though ready to declare that his mother was the cleverest of her sex, he did not think that feminine ability is adapted to inquiries of this sort.

His perfect confidence in Mrs. Acland made Hugh feel the more aggrieved by the withholding of secrets. Those pages torn from the diary were said to be scandals against his mother. If so, they were manifestly absurd, and all the world knew it—

why keep them from him? He persuaded himself that they were not abstracted for that reason. His mother had seen them; but she, in natural haste and indignation, would not observe them closely. Vane, the mutual friend, had probably withdrawn the pages because there was something decisive therein, a hint which would set the question at rest. Anyhow, since they could not possibly harm his mother nor shake his faith in her, he ought to see them. So, after thinking this over, he went back to Paper Buildings for an explanation, at the hour when Vane dressed. That gentleman repulsed him, and they quarrelled.

Returning through Pump Court, Hugh met an old' lady and a young one. At a glance he recognised the tall, lithe figure and graceful head, but the elder lady did not know him. Sternly she asked her way to Paper Buildings, which Hugh gave rather incoherently. The young companion smiled a very little, as they turned away with thanks.

Here was news. But when Hugh mentioned it after dinner, Mrs. Acland was not at all diverted. 'This is the first consequence of your meddling, Hugh!' she said, with an irritation very unusual. 'You have set these people inquiring and annoying. Captain Saxell understood his mother, and he wished to keep her ignorant of the reversionary claim until we had prepared our case at leisure. You have acquainted her with it, and she can urge him by force.'

'How, mother?'

'I don't know the legal form. But Mrs. Saxell can take action to compel the trustees—Major St. Paul, in fact—to execute the will of Sergeant-Major Raikes, or to show cause why they omit to do so in a reasonable time. I had troubles enough before!'

'What were you doing in the Temple, Hugh?' asked Edie. 'Oh, do keep quiet, dear, and leave wiser heads to settle the matter.'

Mrs. Acland's severity had passed. She cried, laughing:

'Apologize to your brother at once, you impertinent girl! Hugh is learning wisdom every day by experience. I could wish he practised it in other people's business, but the desire is laudable. So Mrs. Saxell has come to town! And she is accompanied by the loveliest girl in the world? Tell us about her—is she like Edie?'

'I hope not—not in all respects.'

'Oh, Hugh!'

'I mean that I hope she doesn't bully her brother, if she has one.'

'We never quarrelled in our lives until this horrid news came, and now something is always going wrong. You went to see Mr. Vane?'

'I went to complain to the Lord Mayor that I am not allowed a vote in my own freehold. He said it was monstrous, and if I would bring the obstructive parties before him he would fine them *sine die.*'

'You went to Mr. Vane for some information which you do not like to ask mamma? That is it? "Will you tell me?'

'I don't know anything,' he answered, colouring hotly, 'and I don't wish to know anything but what she tells me.'

'Leave it all to her, dear Hugh, and I will behave so prettily you shall be ashamed to recollect you ever thought of preferring a creature to me.'

'I say, this is serious, little sister? Am I *never*——Nor you?'

'I can speak for myself. I never will! Don't laugh, mamma.'

'Then, to change the conversation, I will give you news. Peake will call on me tomorrow.'

'At what time?' asked Hugh.

'I don't think your presence will be necessary, dear, and it might embarrass the man. I will tell you all that passes.'

Hugh felt still more keenly that he was kept outside of the family interests.

'I shall not go out this evening,' Mrs. Acland continued. 'If you will write a line to Mrs. Palgrave, Edie, she will be pleased to chaperon you, no doubt. And, Hugh, if you are going near the Rhadamanthus I wish you would leave a note for Mr. Vane.'

'To tell him Peake is coming?'

'No, dear; but to consult what can be done to keep Mrs. Saxell quiet.'

'Could I advise you about that?'

'No doubt, and I should be very pleased to discuss the matter. But our talk could not do much good, I fear, unless Mrs. Sax ell has come up to ask your opinion, and will abide by it. I do not understand that you are upon such terms with the lady?'

'I am almost sorry I'm not, mams, if it would lead you to confide in me.'

'Hughie!' exclaimed his sister, in rebuke.

'You will learn to be patient with men, my dear,' said Mrs. Acland pleasantly.

'At least, I hope so, in spite of the decided "I never will," just now. It is a wife's first lesson, and a mother finds it easy. No, my boy; I am not offended in the very least. But you will give Mr. Vane my note?'

'Of course I will, inscrutable but charming mams.'

Two hours later Vane drove up, and he was closeted some time with Mrs. Acland.

'You may depend upon me.' he said, in wishing her good-night. 'It is Saxell's wish, and my own strong conviction, that his mother should not be excited about this affair. She loves money, not for its own sake, but for the pleasure of spending it—of throwing it about, if she had enough. We have an appointment for to-morrow afternoon. I shall urge her to return at once. Your friendly message shall be given. Allow me to say it is just what I should have expected from you. Under happier circumstances, Miss Acland would have found Grace a delightful companion.'

Hugh meantime was playing billiards at the Rhadamanthus with a tall, burly, pleasant-looking youth little older than himself.

'You will change your mind before October, Bob,' he said. 'That's 27, marker.'

'I don't think I shall. It will be an awfully interesting trip. Why don't you come with us?'

'I should like it above everything. Are there elephants there?'

'They're the local equivalent of our rabbit. You bag them at odd moments, when game is out of season. We shall travel leisurely through Ashanti up to this mysterious place, Telaga, shooting as we go, and doing trade enough to pay our expenses. Pringle will push on farther, but he undertakes to accompany me back as far as Coomassie. I have only twelve months' leave, you know.'

'How you will enjoy yourselves! But the country is terribly unhealthy, isn't it?'

'Only on the coast. That's game! Where's Dunscombe to-night?'

'Does anyone know?' asked Hugh. 'I want to see him particularly.'

'Saving errors caused by human frailty and variations of clocks,' said a bystander, 'you'll find him waiting round the corner in his night-cab at a quarter-past eleven.'

'Round what corner? Why in his night-cap?'

'Cab, with a "b," illiterate youth! I don't know exactly what corner, but the one frequented by scions of nobility who haunt the Variety Theatre.'

'Dunscombe is rather forcing the pace there, isn't he?' asked somebody.

'He's distanced all the field! Maud has fallen in love at last!'

'I don't believe it. The news is too bad to be true! Making love to Maud was a public diversion, more innocent than most, and Dunscombe is too good a sportsman to interrupt it. Shooting a fox is venial compared with this.'

'A monstrous expensive diversion, one way and another! He'll effect a public economy if he puts a stop to it!'

'What a mean and unsportsmanlike view to take! Who ever grudged a good fox his goose?'

'You refer to Maud Latham, I suppose?' said Hugh.

'If you take it in that serious tone, I vow I didn't for one!' exclaimed Milroy.

'I didn't mean to be serious. Is she fascinating off the stage?'

'Not a bit!' growled an elderly man. 'Maud Latham is the fashion with a generation of unprincipled idiots, that's all!'

'Who was the fashion in your generation, Blake? The daughter of Herodias?'

'Oh no! Blake's contemporaries didn't dance! They were arboreal in their habits, and the height of fashion was to walk on two legs!'

At the place indicated Hugh found Dunscombe, who looked much annoyed. But his doings were no business of Hugh's, and he resolved more strongly that they never should be.

'I want you to do me an odd service,' he said.

'Reckon it done, and proceed.'

'Will you lend me that shrewd fellow of yours to-morrow?'

'Moore? Certainly!'

'I want him to interview Vane's clerk and find where Mrs. Saxell is staying in town, as I am not on very good terms with Vane.'

'Ah! The loveliest girl in the world accompanies her aunt, I suppose? Are you going to call again?'

'I have no intentions at all beyond discovering where they live.'

'Well, I'll send Moore first thing tomorrow. But you are not the man to content yourself with sighs and envyings, Hugh! Take care.'

A fair girl with large dark eyes came from the direction of the stage-door. Dunscombe raised his hat, put her into the brougham waiting, gave his coachman the name of a restaurant, and bade Hugh good-night.

Moore arrived early, took his instructions without remark, and two hours afterwards returned with the address. Mrs. Saxell was staying at an hotel off Bond Street, of which neither he nor Hugh had ever heard; in truth, the lady had stayed there on her wedding-trip, thirty-five years before; sentiment led her back perhaps, or perhaps she preferred any familiar place among the perils of London. Moore, sent to reconnoitre, brought intelligence that it was quite an 'outside establishment,' as he gravely called it.

'I just threw an eye over the books, sir.

The ladies' rooms are Nos. 64 and 65 on the second-floor. Nos. 63 and 66 are empty, and so is No. 72, just opposite.'

'What an invaluable man you are!' Hugh exclaimed, laughing rather uneasily. 'Lord Dunscombe must prize you.'

'Oh no, sir,' Moore answered, with a respectful smile. 'His lordship doesn't give me any employment in this way.'

'Discreet as sagacious! I feel sure you don't gossip. Take this!'

'Thank you, sir. If there's anything I'm master of, it's my tongue.'

'By-the-bye, what was the number of that empty room opposite?'

'I put it down, sir. No. 72.'

Up to this time Hugh had formed no plans. He did not even purpose consciously to haunt the hotel, though it would have come to that, doubtless. But such matter-of-fact hints produced their result on a young man. Moore took it for granted that he would not' only watch but enter the building; not only enter, but establish himself there, as close to the ladies as possible. Had the suggestion been made directly, Hugh would have been shocked and indignant. But coming as a thing of course, the action which a gentleman might be expected to follow, he entertained it, and that is fatal in such cases. After all, why not?

So, within an hour, Hugh drove up with a portmanteau, and engaged the room; but when he found himself inside, what little impudence dwelt in his honest young soul oozed out. While he hesitated, a door opened opposite, and Miss Palliser's voice was heard in tones of complaint—'Unkind to leave me all alone.'

'It is not fitting for you to accompany me on a business interview. I will be back as early as I can, and, after dinner, we will go to the theatre.'

A moment afterwards the rustle of a dress and the tap of stately feet went down the passage. Then a man came by, and a rattle of plates followed his entrance. Grace spoke again, while the door was open:

'Send the chambermaid, please!'

What she said when the girl went in, Hugh did not hear, but the reply was enough. 'Why, miss,' answered the chambermaid, 'if you turn to the left Bond Street is the third turning; and if you go straight on, you can't mistake Regent Street when you come to it.' Pause and murmur; chambermaid's voice again. 'Yes, miss, but if I was you, I wouldn't go to those streets for a walk, not without your ma. There's the Park now, if you're dull. Turn to the right and keep straight along, it'll bring you there. Young ladies sometimes goes to the Park alone, but not to Bond Street, nor yet Regent Street.'

The chambermaid departed. There's something to be said for these old-fashioned hotels, Hugh thought. A servant at the International or the St. George would not have given number sixty-five good advice as well as service.

It was a long twenty minutes before he heard the door reopen; then light feet pattered down the corridor. He followed presently, lit a cigar in the hall with elaborate unconcern, and stood upon the step to reconnoitre. The graceful form he could not mistake had a hundred yards' advance. Men turned to look after it, but the hateful race of *messieurs qui suivent les femmes* does not abound in those parts of London; and, besides, Grace wore a veil. Hugh almost wished some gigantic scoundrel would address her, that he might introduce himself under a chivalrous aspect. But unmolested Grace walked in maiden innocence, not by any means unaware of admiration, but ignorant of danger or impropriety. She knew that her aunt would disapprove the promenade; but Mrs. Saxell disapproved most actions of young people.

Rhythmic and delightful to observe as is the walk of a girl symmetrically shaped, a young man has difficulty in timing his steps therewith. Knowing the destination, Hugh turned off round a block of houses, struck into Park Lane, and descended as Miss Palliser crossed the road. Upon entering the Park, she hesitated whether to go right or left, but finally turned towards Hyde Park Corner, on the garden-side. Whilst deviously skirmishing anions the trees opposite, Hugh kept her in sight.

When she crossed at the bottom, he made a long leg, reached Rotten Row, and advanced to meet his fate.

The world was at lunch, and few besides nursemaids and country people occupied the path. Hugh had no experience of such adventures, and his heart beat violently, his throat was dry. If Grace did not acknowledge him, or received his bow coldly, he had not courage to address her, though he would have bitterly reproached himself afterwards. When his eager eyes detected her a long way off, Hugh felt almost sick with nervous tremor. But Grace found things dull in London, and her frame of mind was rebellious.

As they drew near she did not pretend unconsciousness. Dissimulation was certainly not numbered among Grace Palliser's many faults, but rashness and heedlessness were. It must be remembered, however, that in the wilds of Scarsholme, where she had dwelt since leaving school, there was little occasion to master the rules of daily conventional etiquette.

Hugh's bow was accepted with a frank little smile, which reassured him forthwith.

'I knew I could not have been mistaken yesterday,' he said, stopping. 'It was Mrs. Saxell who asked me the way to Paper Buildings.'

'Yes. I think I am lost again. Can this be Hyde Park?'

'It is Rotten Row.'

'Rotten Row! I thought all the world crowded there?'

'All the world has gone home to lunch just at present, excepting you and me.'

Hugh had turned, and was walking side by side with his divinity. Grace did not notice anything unusual in his conduct. She said:

'Oh, I don't belong to the world! I came here to take my first peep at it from the outside.'

'Like Moore's Peri.'

'Not at all like Moore's Peri, for I am not disconsolate, and I don't long to enter.'

'And Rotten Row, just now, resembles Paradise only in its solitude.'

'In its freedom from wicked persons, you might have said.'

'That is a prettier way to put it, but it comes to the same thing-, perhaps. If you will accept my escort for an hour you will see the wicked world return.'

'And, if not, shall I be visited with blindness, or will the wicked world stay away? I don't perceive the necessity of your escort, Mr. Acland. And when you remind me of the fact, I know it is not proper to be walking with a gentleman to whom I have not been introduced. Good-morning.'

'If we have not been introduced, Miss Palliser, by what magic do we know each other's names?'

'A question I ought to ask, not you. We are not so inhospitable at Scarsholme as to turn a gentleman out of doors without knowing who he is!'

'A person guided only by that incident would think my name was Adam.'

'Oh!—well, you will admit that a girl should not walk alone with a gentleman she does not know from Adam. Good-morning!'

'Dropping the question of names, it is certain that we do know each other somehow.'

'Rather anyhow,' murmured Grace.

'And I venture to assert that there is less impropriety in walking with a man whose name and position and character you are acquainted with, than alone.'

'Impropriety! "What do you mean?' Grace flushed angrily.

'Only to persuade you to endure my presence,' said Hugh, in alarm.

'Have I done wrong? What a shame that a girl can't walk out on such a lovely day!'

'She can walk as she pleases, under proper escort.'

'But yours is not proper.'

'It is better than none. I am sure Mrs. Saxell would have been pleased to accept it, when she gave you permission to stroll out.'

'What a mischievous——' she stopped.

'But useful man you are,' Hugh added.

'That is not what I was going to say. Mr. Acland, I don't believe this meeting was accidental—answer me upon your honour!'

'I own I followed you from the hotel.'

'How did it happen you were passing the hotel? Upon your honour!'

'What a suspicious character yours is!'

She stopped.

'It was not an accident. I beg you to leave me.'

She did not pretend to be grievously indignant, but her eye was firm enough and her tone. Hugh made some embarrassed explanation.

'You are young and thoughtless,' she answered—' that's the best and the worst I think of you. Now be good enough to let me return alone.'

'I obey. We shall shortly meet under happier auspices.'

'What do you mean by that?'

'At Lord Rainforth's ball.'

'How do you know I am going? you have been asking about me?'

'Dunscombe is my friend; he may possibly have mentioned the grave fact.'

Hugh took off his hat and left her, not quite mistress of the field. She was not hurt perhaps, certainly was not surprised, when, facing on the steps of the hotel, she observed the enemy hovering in the rear, a hundred yards behind.

Hugh's servant called next day to pay his bill and remove the portmanteau. Mrs. Saxell and her niece were in the hall, just leaving. Grace overheard the man's conversation and his master's name. On the long journey to Scarsholme she was silent and not good-tempered—found the day hot, the carriage dusty, the sandwiches tasteless, the milk a criminal compound of chalk and water; remarks all true enough, but original for careless Grace. Mrs. Saxell offered no consolation.

'Remember that I did not ask you to accompany me,' she said.

'I have had all the disagreeables, and I have done no good—that's what irritates me, aunt,' Grace replied. 'If you had let me go with you yesterday Ave should not be returning just as wise as Ave came. I could almost cry!'

'For heaven's sake don't carry your silliness that length! I took you to a theatre, child!'

'Yes, and I am grateful, dear! But we did not go to London for that purpose.'

'It is annoying' and disrespectful, Grace, to keep on in this way. Mr. Vane showed me clearly the uselessness of remaining in town at a great expense. He told me how the case stood, which I hare explained to you. I must say I think Richard quixotic in giving the Aclands so much time to get up their case—making them acquainted with all his evidence, too! Mr. Vane thinks it will cause no difference in the end, but I still think it foolish.'

'For my own part, I don't trust Mr. Vane. Dick doesn't know that he is friendly with the Aclands. I should have insisted on employing my own lawyer.'

'You forget that Richard would not confide in his mother—with the best motives, I hope, but there it is. T trust I have too much pride to interfere.'

'And so we may lose sixty thousand pounds on punctilio? Oh, think if we had sixty thousand pounds!'

'I prefer to think upon more profitable and edifying subjects. I fear the Aclands will feel their loss cruelly. By-the-bye, Mrs. Acland entrusted Mr. Vane with a friendly message. She expressed her deep sense of Richard's consideration and honourable dealing, and said she hoped, however this affair ends, that we should not allow personal animosity to creep in.'

'Oh, I wonder whether she knows you turned her son out of doors? What did you answer?'

'I desired Mr. Vane to say that I appreciated the grace and Christian feeling of her expression. I could do no less, whatever the lady's motive.'

'What motive could she have, besides friendliness and charity? You ought to write to Mrs. Acland, auntie.'

'That would be very injudicious. I must not commit myself; Richard has gone much too far, in my opinion.'

'But I might write.'

'You will do nothing of the sort!'

But Grace had made up her mind on that point. After a while she asked:

'Will young Mr. Acland be ruined if we succeed?'

'I was very glad to learn that he has several thousands a year, independent of Richard's claim. But his sister will lose all her fortune.'

'Poor girl! Is she pretty?'

'I did not ask such a frivolous question.'

After another long pause, Grace said:

'And we must remain in this uncertainty until after the long vacation! How dull it will be waiting at Scarsholme all through the summer and autumn! I shall hate the place!'

'I trust you speak heedlessly. It would be terrible if this prospect of worldly fortune unhinged your mind to that degree. Hate Scarsholme!'

'And the new rosary! Oh, how happy people are who have heaps of money—do what they like, stay in London as long as they please, and go to a theatre every night—like Miss Acland!'

'That is an unfortunate instance. After a youth of frivolity, she may find herself without the means to pursue her career of dissipation, and too probably she has no solid resources to fall back upon.'

'Well, at least she will have lived, not vegetated. You know, auntie, you are just as eager for this fortune as I am; but you won't own it because frankness isn't proper!'

'I prefer silence to scurrilous observations. If Richard gets his own, he will use his means and opportunities for a better purpose than mere enjoyment, I trust.'

'Oh, no doubt. But he will pick up a good deal of mere enjoyment in seeking his better purpose.'

'If he allowed you to guide him, lie would indeed. I am not blind, Grace. I see very well what is passing in your mind.'

'I shall be glad if you will tell me, then, for I thought it was quite empty.'

'This glimpse of London has unsettled you. Your mind, such as it is, was always fixed on luxury, and show, and self-display. You envied every woman, however plain, who had a carriage with a coat-of-arms and a liveried footman. After passing yourself off for a duchess *incognita* at the theatre, you were ashamed when I told the commissionaire to fetch a cab before a dozen impertinent boys dressed out, who waited to see us. You would have given your soul to hear him cry, "Miss Palliser's carriage!" and to go off in a coach and six. I understood very well. It was no discovery that you are mad to join the throng of giddy, vulgar triflers!'

'Indeed I am not, aunt,' Grace began; but her tone was even more startled than indignant.

'I have long been acquainted with your character. Refined pursuits, such as appeal to the artistic sentiment, have no attraction for you. Your utmost wish would be to lead the fashion, however stupid, so long as it was dazzling and costly—to outshine everybody in display, and to secure selfish enjoyment. How far temptation might lead you if it were offered I am distressed to think. Your future gives me many sleepless nights.'

Grace had really been shocked to admit in her own mind that something of this charge might be true. But the sentimental conclusion, so ridiculously false, spoiled all the effect. She laughed.

'I'll try to be a better girl, auntie, if it's only to restore your night's rest—to give my mind, such as it is, to artistic pursuits.'

'You had better,' replied Mrs. Saxell grimly. 'Richard has not means; and if he win the means, he has no inclination to take a show wife.'

'Oh, as for that, he and I will settle those questions between us.'

Mrs. Saxell grunted, not approvingly, and they went to sleep.

CHAPTER V.
THE PEELE HOUSE.

MR. PEAKE is with mamma now,' said Edie, as her brother entered, after his stroll in the Park.

'What is he like?'

'An ugly man. I only caught a glimpse of him.'

'Was the mams agitated, poor darling?'

'I could see she was, but he would not.' They talked while Edie sat working.

'We are good friends now, princess, aren't we?'

'So long as you don't annoy me—quite.'

'Mayn't I speak?'

'Not of her, nor of any of the hateful people. I loathe them—reptiles!'

The word seemed so humorously inaccurate to describe Miss Palliser that Hugh laughed out. His sister flashed a glance at him.

'I ought not to have laughed,' he said penitently. 'Let us talk of something else. Give me your opinion of Dunscombe.'

'It has not changed.'

'I am glad to hear that. Never allow yourself to be persuaded, dear. I do believe that he loves you; but—why, you colour!'

'Girls sometimes do, when brusquely told that gentlemen are in love. But under no circumstances could I get beyond a moderate liking for Lord Dunscombe.'

'Speaking without any reference to him at all, I don't think you are capable of love, Edie. Something like half the gilded youth of England have passed before your eyes, and not one have you looked at twice.'

'Perhaps I don't care for gilded youth; perhaps, as you say, my character is deficient. It doesn't matter much, either way.'

'Oh, was that what you meant last night by saying, "I never will"? Do you think there is no man worthy of you? Mind, little sister, I don't think there are many.'

'There are thousands and millions! It doesn't matter what I mean. No one has shown' the right to ask me at present—no one, that is, who has claimed it.'

'You may stand in another light, princess, if Saxell carries off your fortune.'

'In that point of view, then, I shall not regret the loss.'

'You want a hero, child—just as if you were only sixteen! There are not many heroes about.'

'Then I'll contentedly put up with my silly brother!' she laughed. 'But please understand that I don't want anyone, hero or boor. If I did, he would be something quite different from Lord Dunscombe.'

'We are both agreed on that point. If I had not felt sure, I should not have mentioned his feeling.'

'I am not complimented. Lord Dunscombe is a pleasant acquaintance, and I know no harm of him. But I sometimes think that, if one went much below the surface, one would find ugly depths.—This conversation is very unedifying, Hughie. Let us change it.'

'No; I want to hear your views. No girl is incapable of love, and you least of any. Describe your ideal!'

'Oh dear! I declare I have not the shadow of one! What is the meaning of this cross-examination? Are you trying—I do believe you are——'

'What?'

'To get hints from me for your own use.'

'What an absurd idea! But what then?'

'I don't know what then.'

'There are limits to feminine ingenuity. Now, describe your hero.'

'One need not be modest with one's little brother. I am worth a true man's winning, not without trouble and self-distrust. A true man is brave, and thoughtful, and kind; light-hearted because he is fearless, ready because his intellect is trained, and kind because he is good. I have not analyzed my ideal beyond these points.'

'You have gone quite deep enough to exclude most men. It's lucky that girls in general are not so exacting.'

'I knew you were trying me!'

'Perhaps I want to suggest a friend.'

'Spare us all three I If I could love any man, I don't wish to find him.'

'Have you made up your precious little mind never to marry? It is too absurd!'

'Why? One girl in every three does not marry, as somebody calculates.'

'Girls like you are outside of calculations. But have you made up your mind?'

'There is no need! If I have met my hero, he did not show interest in me, and I did not recognise him. So prepare yourself to see me remain on hand, like a price-less diamond in a shop, which no queen happens to see, and no subject can afford to buy!'

'And which the unbusiness-like jeweller cherishes and' admires so fondly that in his heart he dreads a royal visit, lest the Queen should be tempted. There's a pretty speech for a brother! And all true!'

'You have gleams of reason, my darling Hughie,' said Miss Acland, laughing and blushing. 'The priceless diamond is very happy in its nest, and only afraid that the jeweller will desert it.'

'By-the-bye, I saw Bob Holmes last night. Poor Pringle is really going to seek consolation for his disappointment in West Africa.'

'I am very sorry for Major Pringle. He is a noble fellow. Surely West Africa is a dreadful country to travel in!'

'Bob wanted me to join them, and I should have been awfully tempted had I been free. The climate is healthy when you leave the coast.'

'You would not have had the heart to abandon us, Hughie!'

'I don't know! Think of the excitement and the novelty! Here comes the mams! Well, dear?'

'The interview has been painful, but conclusive, I hope. Don't ask any questions yet, dear Hugh.'

Her children comforted her with loving words and kisses.

'I think I shall not have to see him again,' said Mrs. Acland. 'Will you ring the bell, Hugh? If Edie can go with me, I should like a drive.'

'I am not invited?' Hugh asked, laughing, but rather sore.

'Not because I do not love you as well, my son,' Mrs. Acland exclaimed with emphasis. 'You are both equally dear to me. But Edie will sit quiet and still, giving me only a little pressure of the hand and a look; you would shuffle and talk and kindly try to distract me—in short, you would be a kind, good son, and you would bring me home more tired than I set out.'

'Had ever man such a charming, false, dear, Machiavelian mother! There! I will leave you to feminine wiles and consolations. Good-bye, sweetest mams!'

He went to seek Dunscombe. After employing a man's servant in dubious ways, the merest courtesy exacts that an account be given. So Hugh said to himself, but in fact he was influenced as much by the longing to talk things over with an experienced friend. It was not heroic, but none of my characters make that pretension. They have no more of the delicacy or chivalry we read about than other people. Hugh's feeling towards Grace was far below the point of intensity which forbids a youth to name the object of his pure love. The fun and excitement of the chase still counted for much, and he told his story with humour.

'Upon my soul,' said Dunscombe, 'when you move you go apace! This is the young fellow who rebukes simple-minded men like me!'

'The cases are utterly different,' said Hugh, with sudden gravity. 'But we are not going to discuss yours. I have the Countess's invitation for the ball. A thousand thanks, Dunscombe. Has Mrs. Saxell accepted, do you know?'

'Of course. We are all going up next Friday to arrange for welcoming Ralph with due honour at Daneham. If you have nothing better to do, come with us.'

Hugh consented gladly, and in due time found himself in a railway carriage with Lady Rainforth and her daughter Madge; Carruthers, to whom that young lady was engaged; General the Hon. George Randall and his wife; Paul Randall, a cousin, and Dunscombe.

Lord Rainforth prided himself on being a Dalesman. After a stormy youth and a penitent middle-age, he had settled, philosophic and contented, in the old home, among grey fells waist-deep in bracken, sunny copses of oak and birch, dark pine woods. Neither wife nor children dwelt with him, now that Ralph had married. Lady Rainforth argued that as she had borne no part in the errors deplored, she could not be justly called upon to share the penance; and her husband accepted this reasoning. But all paid frequent visits to Daneham, and the family met upon kindly terms. Lord Rainforth preferred his second son, observing too many of his own foibles in the elder. When Dunscombe was a very young 'sub' in India, he had been named extra A.D.C. to the Viceroy, and his prospects were excellent. But he fell into one of those blatant scandals which cannot be overlooked, though charitable persons scarcely blame a boy who is the victim. In self-reproach and anger, Dunscombe sent in his papers, and returned to lead an utterly useless life at home.

Hugh had met all his companions saving the General, but they appeared in a new character to-day—the old ladies frank and motherly; Lady Madge still tired with last night's ball, but willing to be amused; the young men in high spirits.

Lady Rainforth observed to Hugh: 'You are warned that you will meet foes on our neutral ground?'

'Mrs. Saxell and Miss Palliser have nothing to do with the question.'

'Has Grace turned out as pretty as she promised?' asked Mrs. Randall. Dunscombe's lips mutely framed 'The loveliest girl in the world!' but the General replied:

'If she promised she has kept her word better than most young ladies do. But you are wrong, Mr. Acland, in thinking that she has no interest in Captain Saxell's claim. It is an act of charity to warn all you young civilians that Miss Palliser has chosen the long sword, saddle, bridle, and all the other accoutrements of the honest soldier!'

'Dear me!' exclaimed his wife, 'all the accoutrements—already?'

'I allude to the ornamental ones, my dear, sung by poets.'

'But the poet has sung of certain other imminent and deadly togs, in express allusion to the soldier,' murmured Carruthers.

'His advice to your sort, sir, was to pen your mistress's eyebrow. Go do it, and don't blaspheme.'

'Oh, let me pen your eyebrow, Madge! It is my duty! Countess, use your authority!'

'You have set this silly young man's brain whirling, General. He will talk of penning my eyebrows for a week.'

Whilst all were laughing and chatting gaily, Hugh sat aghast. Dunscombe observed him, and said:

'You don't tell us who the lucky soldier is, General?'

'Captain Saxell, of course—Major Saxell, Y.C., I should say—the hero of Abdallah Karez and the pride of our county. Here's last night's " Gazette!" Promotion and the Cross in one number. That's glory—and luck!'

'I remember him as a boy,' said Lady Rainforth. 'He was full of spirit and fun.'

'We saw him in India,' observed Mrs. Randall. 'It was at a dâk bungalow somewhere.'

'At Mhow, my dear, when we were going to Gwalior. He had tiffin with us.'

'I remember him very well. A hand some figure of a soldier, full of spirits—though he had trouble enough you told me, General.'

'Poverty was his only complaint, my dear. Although he is opposed to our young friend in a matter of business, I must say I love Dick Saxell.'

'If the brave deserve the fair,' said Lady Rainforth, 'he and Grace Palliser are well matched.'

'If!' exclaimed Carruthers—'do you throw doubt on the poet's authority? Madge will never let me pen her eyebrows now, and life becomes a weary blank.'

With such composure as he could summon, Hugh observed:

'They told us Major Saxell had been eight or ten years in India.'

'Something like it. He went out with St. Paul, who has commanded the battery since—let me see—1873, I think.'

'And he has not been home?' Lady Madge exclaimed. 'Grace is only eighteen now. He must have won her heart by letter.'

'Proposed through the post, as Pyramus did to Thisbe,' cried Carruthers.

'I should scarcely call it an engagement under the circumstances,' Dunscombe said. 'Suggestion is the strongest word appropriate. There's a chance for gay civilians yet, General!'

'Not against this!' cried the old warrior, waving his 'Gazette' triumphantly. '*This* will defeat your heartless schemes to rob the war-worn soldier of his bride! What are your airs and graces beside her Majesty's public acknowledgment of a man's valour, judgment, and—good fortune? Crawl into holes and hide yourselves, you young landloupers and counter-jumpers, when the successful soldier clanks by!'

'My dear General, you carry an old joke too far.'

'No! We are all Randalls here except Carruthers, who has taken advantage of the family degeneracy. Where is the soldier amongst them? Don't interrupt! an old man of the last generation, who has not been luck}T, though he—I won't be interrupted, Martha! There's Dunscombe, our future chief! He began life like a Randall, but—what do you say? Oh, I beg ten thousand pardons, Mr. Acland! We were talking so freely and pleasantly that I forgot you were not one of the family.'

'I am flattered, General! Pray don't bring me clown to my level by an apology!'

'Level be handed, sir! If it comes to that, what I said about a Randall applies to an Acland. Why is an Acland a civilian?—I mean the head of the house. I knew your grandfather and your great-uncle—they were soldiers. I often met your father. If he had lived and prospered you would have been one of us, no doubt; but loafing Randalls and others of the sort have corrupted you.'

'Dear General, we don't mind you at all; but may I point out that my mother is trying to go to sleep, and that Madge is softly dreaming?'

'This would be a favourable opportunity to pen her eyebrow, don't you think?'

'Oh, go to sleep, cuckoo!'

Silence for an hour; then intervals of wakefulness, for casual refreshment, and more light talk. Hugh did his best to take part in it, but he was miserable. The announcement that Grace was engaged, and lost to him, suddenly stirred his amused admiration into hot love. Unreasonable, but very natural.

In the afternoon they reached Preston, where the Earl was waiting—a big, clear-eyed, white-whiskered chieftain. He shook hands with the General, nodded all round, kissed his daughter, and carried off her ladyship for a drive tête-à-tête.

I have hinted that Lord Rainforth was an eccentric philosopher. 'You will not be introduced till this evening,' Dunscombe whispered to his friend. 'There are some family regulations I must explain.'

Daneham Castle lies about ten miles from Preston, a house as pleasant as may be found in the pleasant North-country. No trace of Gothic does it show, saving the Peele House at the back, a memorial of times when Randall was no better than Elliot or Forster or Armstrong. Not once nor twice had the head of the family been suspended over that massive portal, before a canny Randall came to power who profited by the warning, and sought less dangerous means of prosecuting ends identical. That he and his successors did not search in vain is proved by the stately pile which masks their antique donjon. The Italian architect who designed it, in the middle of the last century, wept and raged when forbidden to demolish the Peele House. He declared it a 'naughtiness,' a shameless crime. But the Rainforth of the day was firm. Remonstrations could not move his barbaric soul, and sarcasm he met with oaths. So the Peele House was not touched. It could not be made to harmonize with the reproduction of some Grand Ducal palace in Tuscany, and the architect did his best to hide it behind the central block of his palatial castle.

Whilst Lord Rainforth and the others alighted at the Italian portico, Dunscombe and Hugh drove on, past the facade and the west wing, and drew up at the squat old gateway of the Tower.

'You must know,' said Dunscombe, alighting, 'that the heir-apparent has occupied this original seat of our family since the castle was built. As soon as a Dunscombe comes of age, he takes up these quarters, and there he entertains whom he pleases, subject to rules which I must explain.'

The grim and hoary arch had been made as cheerful as circumstances allowed with Indian matting, bright tiles, flowers and hangings; but it was very old-world still. A narrow slit on either side gave admittance to a vault-like corridor, with nooks in the thickness of the wall, to shelter a few desperate defenders when the gates were forced. The chambers to which it led, and the dungeons at the back, were used by servants, and for storage. A straight, steep staircase ascended from the guard-room to the great hall, where it ended abruptly behind a screen of modern raising. Following Dunscombe through the doorway of carved oak, Hugh stood in admiration. The hall was of no great size, though it occupied all the area of the building. At this floor the ancient staircase had been cut away, and its 'well' marked by the screen referred to. In the space gained by destruction of the massive wall and steps, two large Tudor windows, commanding a delightful scene, lighted the whole apartment, which had been dark at summer noon when dependent on the narrow meurtrières. They now were filled with glass, of colours pale and subdued, but deep enough to shut out the Italian palace. By either side of each stood a suit of armour, not dusty and loose-jointed, but gleaming as on a day of battle, and set in attitudes easy and significant. And everything about the room was, or seemed to be, in harmony with those antique trophies; even the lounging-chairs, of winch the springs and cushions had been cunningly fitted upon antique frames. The tables shining like black mirrors, the cabinets, the pictures, the flower-pots, even the ash-trays and cigar-stands, were genuine bits of moyenage, fitted sometimes to another use. The only things modern, but these not incongruous, were the stairs of beaten brass which wound spirally upward, and the carpets of Turkestan; which latter, being Oriental, differed but in age from those that a Randall Crusader might have brought from the Holy Land.

'It is the most perfect thing I ever saw!' Hugh exclaimed. 'All so elegant and bright, though grave! You must have passed years in Wardour Street!'

'Oh, so many Dunscombes had given their minds to furnishing the Peele House there was little for me to do! Come and see your room!'

They mounted the brazen steps to a floor above, divided into six rooms, small, but as prettily modern as Gothic windows and three-foot walls will allow. Above this were servants' rooms.

'There's time for a cigarette and a brandy and soda without killing your appetite,' said Dunscombe, as they returned to the hall. 'I must make you acquainted with the rather curious usages of our family. You understand that this tower belongs to the Dunscombe of the moment. His guests are his own; he may or may not introduce them over the way, and the Lord Rainforth of the moment may or may not recognise them. Although the governor and I have never had an unfriendly word, he is a stickler for precedent, and he keeps up all the formalities. I shall presently take you across and introduce you, and he will, ask you to dinner. I shall mention that you are staying some days, and he will solemnly express a hope that whenever I honour his table you will accompany me. The first time you see him, every day, you will remind him of this standing invitation; and he will graciously assure you of welcome, Vary the form as ingeniously as you can; the dear old fellow likes niceties of that sort.'

'How very droll and curious!'

'For exceptional entertainments you will receive a special invitation; to the ball you are already asked. Then, you must tell your servant not to enter the front door; even if you forget while in the castle, and send for him, he must not do it. He may go to the servants' hall, and anywhere at the back, as much as he pleases. Under no circumstances must you ask a person staying at the castle into this tower. If you want to do so, you must apply to me and I will invite him, after asking my father's permission.

'These rules seem odd, but they were all devised at one time or another by the practical experience of our ancestors, and a story hangs to each of them. That forbidding Dunscombe to invite Rainforth's guests without his knowledge and consent dates from a tragic legend which I will tell you one day. Now I think you are posted, and it is time to dress.'

'The General has taken away my appetite,' said Hugh dismally.

'Oh, the rivalry of a man in India, not seen for eight years, is not very alarming!'

They went to the house together, entering by a side-door.

'This walk,' said Dunscombe, 'is the objection to a very pleasant arrangement. For generations we have talked of covering it in, but when Dunscombe becomes Rain-forth he always fears the innovation.'

Even intimate acquaintance with great nobles in London scarcely prepares a man to behold them with indifference arrayed in all their glory at home. Barring an unconscious disregard of money, and a matter-of-fact luxury in details, it had not struck Hugh that Dunscombe was remarkable amongst young men of gentlemanly position. Now it suddenly came home to him what a grand personage is an English lord of ancient birth and fortune. Not the superb house nor the train of servants impressed him much—a lucky financier has these things as splendid. It was the careless sense of continuity with ancestors in mail and wig, the allusion to historic names and deeds *quorum pars magna fuit* every Randall and every Dunscombe, in the person of his forefathers. Hugh was a gentleman by birth, of ancient lineage. His name and his forefathers were not unknown; but they had served in the ranks, as it were, whither this kingly race had led.

'We have the portrait of an Acland in our gallery,' said Dunscombe. 'She married—I forget; the governor knows, perhaps. Ah, if your sister could be influenced by the precedent, how diligently would I get it up!'

When they reached the drawing-room the ceremonies indicated were duly performed. It was a small dinner. The elder ladies did not appear, few of the house-guests had arrived, and for such a late entertainment no one of the neighbourhood had been invited. Hugh sat next to General Randall, who said:

'Dunscombe has asked me to smoke my cheroot in his quarters to-night. 'I am pleased to make acquaintance with the third generation of your family. Is the shooting at Worstan kept up as it used to be?'

'Come and report, sir. You knew my father, then?'

'Slightly. Your great-uncle commanded the 100th when I joined. He was on good terms with his brother then, your grandfather. Hugh's death was very sad. How is Mrs. Acland?'

'Do you know her, too?'

'Didn't the wedding take place in my drawing-room? She has never mentioned that? Ay, sad to think of now! Sad story altogether!"

Hugh did not show the astonishment he felt. 'My mother,' he said, 'does not allude to those times willingly. I have heard very little about them. Will you tell me all you can think of?'

'It's very little, but you're welcome to what I remember.'

When dinner ended. Dunscombe ceremoniously asked permission of his father to entertain the General. It was granted j and whilst the other gentlemen adjourned to billiards, these three withdrew to the Peele House.

'No alterations, eh? No new old pots or kettles? You spend your pocket-money less innocently.'

'Improvement is not possible, surely!' said Hugh.

'Humph! Upon these matters the opinion of the elder and the younger generation seldom coincide. Put in another form, Rainforth seldom approves of Dunscombe's proceedings. And that brings us to the subject of your family, Mr. Acland. I've been trying to recall my memories of your father,' the General continued, thoughtfully inspecting his cheroots. 'He was a baby when I first saw him at Worstan, and little more when I went to India. What a fuss everybody made over the heir! And they tell me that not a soul troubled himself to ascertain whether he was living or dead twenty-five years later! There's a moral in that.'

'I observed, in my short military career,' said Dunscombe, 'that field-officers are always immensely interested in morals—O Lord, -what a slip! I hit the blot myself, General! In mercy spare us a play on words!'

The General answered only with a look.

'I recollect meeting your father in 1855, "when I took leave from India. He was at Oxford then—a fine, dashing young fellow. It was Acland's great misfortune that he did not enter the service. That would have smoothed him over. Your family are knotty, very—that is, they were.'

'You said that my father was married in your house. How did that happen?'

'Ah, it was a chain of circumstances, of which I can tell you only a little bit. I got home again in August of the Mutiny year, fell in love on the voyage, and, as soon as I recovered, chose hunting-quarters within reach of the lady. £To need to look at me, Dunscombe! You are very well acquainted with her, for she is my wife. I took a box by Lay stone, of a man named Beaver. One day the parson called with a note from him, saying that he had promised to allow Hugh Acland to be married in his drawing-room; but it was found inconvenient, and would I lend them a corner somewhere? You will guess that I had a kind of unreasoning sympathy for young folks in that position, but I refused to hear of it without the authority of Acland's parents. The parson urged me, and then your father came. He showed a letter of my friend Pete's (that was your great-uncle), which, so far as I remember, told him pretty well to go to the devil his own way, and enclosed a cheque for a wedding-present. I have hinted that Pete and his brother, your grandfather, were on bad terms then. I wrote to both of them, and neither answered. So, to cut the matter short, your father and mother were married one day in the parlour of my cottage. Beaver and I and an old woman were the witnesses, and we all wore pink and tops—that is, the men did. After the ceremony we rode to the meet, had a fine run, and got home for a wedding dinner. It was all your father's idea, and a good one. You might have thought it was no marriage at all, but just a gathering of old friends for a domestic *tableau vivant,* so to speak. The oddest and the prettiest wedding I ever saw, but Martha wouldn't consent to follow the example. What a charming woman Mrs. Acland was—is still, I'll be bound, for hers is a type that lasts! Your father was a handsome man too. I didn't see them afterwards, I think. So that's all I can tell you.'

'I'm very much obliged to you, General. The clergyman's name was Hardwicke, I suppose?'

'Hardwicke it was, of course. A lively fellow for a parson—full of spirits, I mean. Pie made us all laugh with his speech after dinner.'

'Did you see much of your landlord, Beaver?'

'Not much. I dined once at Beaverlowe with the most extraordinary crowd of lunatics you could find in an asylum. There were all sorts and all conditions of men, but all mad. Beaver himself was too clever by half—one of those fellows you don't know where to have. It always seems an odd thins; to me how well I recollect that man. though I saw so little of him.'

'So fast or so dull?' asked Dunscombe.

'That wasn't it either way. What I seem to remember is his queerness; but he rode like a devil. Perhaps it was his wealth and old blood that struck me, when such an odd chap carried them, you know. But I really couldn't say much about Beaver. He was above my understanding, and I didn't see more of him than could be helped, after making up my mind to that. Is he alive?'

'I believe so. We hope he will be able to give valuable evidence in the case.'

'I trust you will find him a willing witness then, for I fancy Beaver would be awkward to drive. Now, you young fellows are going to make a night of it, I suppose? Very proper at your time of life, but at mine we prefer the daylight while we can enjoy it.'

When they were alone, Dunscombe asked how the suit was progressing, and Hugh frankly told what he knew. In the narrative it became disagreeably apparent to himself what large gaps his ignorance was compelled to leave, and the other's questions irritated him. Again, bit by bit, Hugh's grievances came out—how the inquiry seemed to be carried on above his head, how there were secrets, how parts of Raikes's diary had been suppressed by Vane with Mrs. Acland's concurrence. When all had been told, Dunscombe himself rebuked the imprudence.

'You really must learn,' he said, with kindly gravity, 'to control that frank tongue of yours, Hugh! With me there's no harm done, of course, for I'm almost as much interested as if the case was my own. But the other side might be very pressing to know what was in those papers suppressed.'

'Why, Vane suppressed them with Saxell's - knowledge!' Hugh exclaimed; but he already felt his silliness.

'Saxell, I understand, is a chivalrous sort of enemy, but he's not the only one. I've been talking to people who know his mother, and what they tell of her leads me to think that she won't stand on chivalry when her time comes. Take my advice! I've learned some prudence in hard schooling, Hugh. If I'd not been as honest as you are now, I shouldn't be fretting my life away, ruined by a woman. That knocks the innocence out of a man, with a vengeance! Don't say one word about your business to anybody here—not even to the General. He's a fine old soldier, but old soldiers who have nothing to do are the worst mischief-makers on earth. Now let's change the conversation!'

CHAPTER VI.
AN ESCAPADE.

To fashionable persons summoned from town in the waning height of the season, beauties of nature appeal in vain. Among the victims brought down by Lady Rainforth in her suite, a general sense of ill-usage rose so early as next day. No preparations had been made for their amusement beside, as Dunscombe put it, a rapturous imagining of Ralph's return, beatified and married. Lord Rain-forth thought he had done all the duty of a host when he had conscientiously inspected the stable, the larder, and the cellar of a morning. After that, he vanished till dinner-time, and Dunscombe made no effort to replace his father. As the breadth and grandeur of the festivity designed became more evident, his discontent swelled visibly.

Upon the third day, at breakfast, Carruthers raised his voice.

'Dear Lady Rainforth,' he began, 'as a disinterested party, I am commissioned to beg that you will find some pleasing mischief for these young men to do. Their hands are idle, and they have been brought up in the fear of the Evil One. Couldn't you ask some of the ladies invited to the ball to come a few days earlier?'

'I should think Mrs. Saxell and Grace might be tempted, mamma!' said Madge.

'We will carry the invitations!' Grisain exclaimed. 'The General will sketch out a plan, and we irresponsible bachelors will execute his strategy. Carruthers—oh, Carruthers will head the assault with his smile. Ladies yield at discretion to his smile.'

'Prudent boys tremble at his frown! Remember, dear Lady Rainforth, that you will at least be rid of these offensive youths until dinner-time.'

'It is worth while to try, dear. Write notes to'——Mrs. This and Miss That, with whom our story has no concern.

The young men rode away in high spirits. The cottage at Scarsholme was their first point of attack; Hugh made an excuse, and waited at the inn. When they re-turned,, with Mrs. Saxell's assent, they had a theme for rhapsody which lasted the afternoon.

'If manhood suffrage was not an empty farce,' said Grisain, 'Miss Palliser would be elected member for the county.'

'She is worthy of a House to herself, I should think! How gladly would I give her mine, with all the worldly goods that a pernicious monetary system has left me!' cried Phil Randall.

'We would make her jeime Première of an adoring party,' continued Grisain.

'I dare say she would prefer the Home Office,' said Dunscombe.

And all agreed that Miss Palliser was the loveliest girl in the world. Dunscombe smiled at Hugh as he added, 'Excepting one!'

'Excepting one!' hastily interposed Carruthers.

'Excepting one!' Grisain murmured, in romantic reverie.

'Oh, I except one too, for the sake of harmony!' grumbled Philip.

'And I don't except any at all beneath the angels!' cried Hugh.

All looked at him, and laughed.

'Why, you——' began Carruthers, and paused.

'Didn't——' softly continued Phil.

'See her!' ended Grisain meditatively.

'I trust your unanimous judgment!' Hugh said.

They absently exclaimed 'Oh! that's it!' one after another, and dropped the subject.

Hugh's heart beat violently as he entered the drawing-room next day. Instinct guided his eye amongst the ladies present, and the first person he saw was Grace, seated by her aunt. After paying Lord Rainforth the compliments rigorously expect-ed every evening, he was quite overcome by nervousness; but Dunscombe took his arm, pinching it severely, and led him up to the encounter. Mrs. Saxell, forewarned, recognised her visitor with a strong look of displeasure.

Madge, General Randall, and Carruthers, whom Dunscombe had made accom-plices, executed a strategic movement which covered the operation, and his lord-ship assumed a diplomatic tone.

'I am taking a liberty, Mrs. Saxell, which your generous nature will understand, if it cannot approve. Loyal and chivalrous enemies are the best friends off the battle-field. I wish to make known to each other two persons whom all of their acquaintance esteem. Let me present to you Mr. Hugh Acland.'

A dozen emotions had passed visibly across the old lady's face, but Dunscombe's speech, carefully framed and rehearsed, resolved them all to grim acquiescence. How could she remain hostile when credited with loyal and chivalrous sentiments?— how explain that she had turned out of doors a friend of Lord Dunscombe? Mrs. Saxell smiled acidly and bowed.

Then Grace had not told her of the meeting in Hyde Park! Immensely relieved, Hugh made his speech in turn.

'I beg you, Mrs. Saxell, to obliterate a recollection of which I am deeply ashamed. With all my heart I congratulate the mother of a noble foe upon the honours he has won.'

'Your remarks are very gracefully turned, sir,' said Mrs. Saxell, relenting; they should be, Dunscombe thought, when he took an hour polishing them. 'I willingly forget the occurrence; and I am obliged to your lordship for giving me an oppor-tunity to thank Mr. Acland for the kind message his mother sent us through Mr. Vane.'

Dinner was announced; Dunscombe offered his arm.

'Will you take Miss Palliser, Hugh?' he said.

During this time Grace had held herself ostentatiously outside the conversa-tion, showing the whitest, pearliest of shoulders, but the coldest too.

'I have not—er—hum!' murmured Hugh.

'Will you carry your kindness—er—hum?' murmured Dunscombe to Mrs. Saxell.

'Grace, my love, Mr. Hugh Acland offers you his arm.'

She looked up with such freezing power in her eyes that Hugh shivered. The others turned—all the room was moving. Those only remained still; Hugh speech-less.

'I will take your arm,' said Grace, rising, 'but not in sign of forgiveness.'

'You can never say anything so hard as I have said to myself.'

'You have said nothing to yourself so hard as you deserve. I did not know then what a horrid insult you put upon me. I have asked since.'

'My conduct was foolish and indelicate, but surely if it had been wilfully insulting you would have felt it so before others told you.'

This argument seemed to strike Miss Palliser. She sat down without reply.

'I was so pleased to hear of Captain Saxell's promotion and his cross.'

Grace said nothing, but ate her soup with a frank enjoyment unusual but delicious to observe. 'I wish I was *that* spoon!' thought Hugh.

He tried again.

'Your stay in London was very short.'

'It gave me some experience.'

'Which longer acquaintance would possibly not confirm. Grievous mistakes are made upon insufficient knowledge.'

'A slight knowledge contents me, and it matters very little whether I make mistakes or not.'

'Be merciful!' Hugh whispered. 'I implore you to believe in my penitence.'

She threw a keen look into his eyes, and softly laughed.

'I quite believe you don't like snubbing. There! I forgive, because it is not worth while to resent.'

After that they chatted very smoothly and gaily. Grace did not conceal her interest in the dinner, which she criticized with dainty science. Hugh's ignorance diverted her.

'Don't you love nice things?' she said. 'I adore them all—dress and flowers and jewellery—in short, all that money will buy. I was born wicked, and no one has succeeded in converting me.'

'Any change would be for the worse!' exclaimed Hugh enthusiastically.

'You mean by that foolish speech that my personal appearance meets with your approval. I was referring to my character, of which you know less than nothing.'

'Less than nothing!'

'Yes, for what you think you know is all wrong.'

'Will you enlighten my ignorance?'

'I am egotistical enough to do so—that's one point. I am extravagant, frivolous, really incapable of thought—unless like a savage, for some object visible and strongly desired. Then I am as inquisitive as a monkey; selfish—but I can't remember all the list at once.'

'And the good points?'

'They are all qualified by a negative condition. I am good-tempered, so long as nothing puts me out. I am kind-hearted, when not asked to take trouble or to sacrifice my own pleasure. I am liberal and forgiving, because I can't look far ahead nor far behind. And courageous, because I am a Daleswoman.'

'I have listened attentively, but I do not see the weight of your self-accusation. All the bad qualities you claim are shared by nine hundred and ninety-nine girls in a thousand; and statistics tell us that the remaining one is an idiot.'

'Oh, thank you! It is such a relief to find that one is thoroughly commonplace and ordinary!'

'I said that your evil qualities were shared by all other women. Your virtues are your own.'

'But when I tell you I have none!'

'It proves that you have frankness and modesty—which are two to begin with. You must know a few girls. Are many angelic!'

'No; most of them are silly and cowardly.'

'Then you have two more virtues above the girls of your acquaintance. Two pairs and a flush is considered a good hand at poker.'

'You mean that I should do fairly as a housemaid? We dilute truth in these parts.'

'No, indeed! I hazarded a little jest drawn from the fashionable game of cards. It meant that a player blest with your hand would face any fortune.'

'You have an unfair advantage/ answered Grace, laughing and blushing. 'I don't know the game. It is one that seems to lend itself to equivoque.'

'Therefore is it called "poker"—an instrument proper to the cheery fireside, but the readiest of weapons in a fray.'

'Please express your wit in the terms of cribbage; there I can follow you.'

'Then I decline. There is a hostile science in your tone, and I feel "one for my nob" already threatening. Let us resume the former subject, which had a balmy fascination for both. You are not more wicked than is becoming, Miss Palliser.'

'Your impertinent rattle amuses me. Frankly, Mr. Acland, I didn't think you so ready. We didn't observe the quality at Scarsholme.'

'Not many actors could double the part of Coriolanus with Romeo.'

'I don't understand! But please spare me the explanation. I'll look it up. Lord Rainforth has Dr. Johnson's works, I suppose.'

'Coriolanus is not Johnson's. It was composed by W. Shakespeare Thackeray, music by Sir John Smarto.'

'Oh, thank you! But even in the Park you were not really droll—not intentionally, I mean.'

'A man is not intentionally droll when he is frightened to death. But I fondly thought I had some pleasing conceits.'

'I observed the conceit. It was not pleasing in my opinion. Tell me now, Mr. Acland, how did you find out where we were staying? Did Mr. Vane tell you?'

'Does the homing pigeon consult a weather-cock? Instinct guides him in a manner he cannot explain—at least, I never heard a pigeon give a lucid and categorical analysis of his method.'

'I am quite serious in asking this. When I forgave you, it slipped my memory. But I expect an answer.'

'Upon your own head be it, then! Is your modesty so unsuspicious that you think people would not notice you passing, nor speak of you afterwards? I am afraid, Miss Palliser, you will find it difficult to preserve *incognito* in London. It may be done in these parts, but not in an appreciative centre of civilization.'

'Oh! Then the policeman at the corner, or a friend at the Club, or somebody told you!'

'I may answer, "Yes." '

'You may answer anything. We will change the conversation. Are you Lord Rainforth's guest or Lord Dunscombe's?'

'Dunscombe's, and we live disconsolate at the Peele House.'

'So I thought. Now, you wish to merit forgiveness, as I understand?'

'I merit it already, by all Protestant doctrines.'

'By faith? It is always an error, I believe, to try to rule mankind, and more especially womankind, by theological dogma. I insist upon works in profane matters. Persuade Lord Dunscombe to give a tea-party at the Peele House. He does sometimes—that is, he has done so.'

'It is a small request, and one that does not depend on me. Impose something greater.'

'I shall be quite satisfied and forgiving if you succeed. I have never seen the Peele House—oh dear, there's Lady Rain-forth signalling, and I have not sipped this delicious claret; now that opportunity is lost! How disappointing life is!'

With a rustle of dresses the ladies rose to leave, but Dunscombe arrested the movement. He said:

'The gardener begs Lord Rainforth to let him know what colours or combinations are desired in the bouquets he has to furnish for Thursday. 'If every gentleman will note down the ideas of the lady next him we shall get the information in two minutes.'

'What is your notion, Miss Palliser?' Hugh asked.

'Oh, my bouquet should be white and flimsy, to match Dacca muslin. As transparent as possible. Tea-roses, azaleas, if he has any left; and trimmed with two tints in blue, light and dark.'

'I quite understand. Whether the resources of botany run to two shades of blue is the gardener's question.'

'Any respectable milliner would supply me with two hundred! Don't profanely suppose that Nature has a more limited stock.'

'It is the milliner's business, you know, to meet ladies' fancies.'

'And what do you suppose flowers are intended for?'

'I haven't the faintest notion,' he replied. 'Perhaps they are meant to suit the fancies of humble bees.'

'What a wicked thought! Humble bees know their place better. Wild flowers are quite good enough for them, but woman must have variety and choice. The wonders of horticulture are meant for us.'

When the ladies withdrew, Dunscombe moved to the bottom of the table and signalled Hugh to take a place beside him. The notes were handed in, with pleasant comments.

'It seems to me,' said Dunscombe, 'that Miss Palliser has the most distinct idea what she wants. I could arrange the bouquet myself.'

'I hope she may get it,' murmured Hugh.

'Is it all made up?' Dunscombe whispered.

'The offence? Yes. It was only skin-deep.'

'Well then, be satisfied! I have been watching you, my boy. Don't get beyond your depth.'

'Why not? It's mighty pleasant swimming.'

'You may easily push out too far to return. Miss Palliser is a born flirt, Hugh, and these unconscious man-eaters are the most dangerous.'

'Miss Palliser is not unconscious. Far from it.'

'I'm glad you can regard her critically. Leave it to Saxell, among your other ill-wishes for him, to verify the analysis.'

'What has prejudiced you against her?'

'I thought this was all fun, as innocent for you as I'll be bound it is for Miss Palliser. But it seems to me that you are getting serious, and I don't like it.'

'Why?'

'In the first place, this young lady is engaged.'

'You said yourself that the engagement must be a force.'

'In one sense, but you have nothing to do with that. In your interest I have been talking to Lady Seagrim, who is clever but not malicious. Miss Palliser can count her scalps in this neighbourhood. She lends herself to any degree of admiration, but when a young fellow follows the natural course, after so much encouragement, she is very much surprised, rather hurt, and thinks it an impertinence. So Lady Seagrim tells me. Miss Palliser is what I call an innocent man-eater. She wants to make a match as big as you please—not consciously, I dare say, but that's what her instincts point to. I have seen girls enough to recognise the style. Take warning.'

'I know you mean kindly, Dunscombe, and I'm obliged. But don't outrage common-sense by telling me you have seen one other girl like Miss Palliser. Honestly now?'

'I have seen but one handsomer—that's what you mean, I suppose? But the character is not at all uncommon, if you will allow me to think so. Now I've said my say, and you will profit or you won't. These men will begin to think we are conspiring.'

'By-the-bye, Miss Palliser is anxious to see the Peele House.'

'I'm not in the humour for tea-parties. At her next visit.'

Dunscombe rose, and led his friends to the smoking-room for a cigarette. Hugh joined the ladies at once, and told Grace the result. She flushed with annoyance, and said sharply:

'How could you have put it to be refused? Every girl in the county has had an invitation without asking!'

'Dunscombe was more in the humour for tea-parties then, I suppose. It's a merry frame of mind which certainly doesn't possess him just now. There's something noxious in the air of Daneham just now, as it seems to me; and the best of dispositions give way to injustice and violence. We shall live through it, Miss Palliser, under a treatment of philosophy and tonics.'

'Do you hint a reproach at me, sir? Oh, chivalry! what are we coming to? I have a right to be angry, Mr. Acland, and I will avenge myself.'

'I should not dare to question your right. But a young lady's vengeance, as I have always understood, is an explosive of the deadliest character, which plays the mischief in all directions. I will undertake to find Dunscombe in a better temper if you can be patient for a few hours.'

'Don't ask him again on any account! I should be seriously angry, Mr. Acland—or rather, let me say, I should be humiliated. It's very well as it is. We shall see.'

The next day, after lunch, Lord Rainforth mustered all his guests of the Randall name, to welcome the bride and bridegroom at Preston. Hugh was witness to the struggle that Dunscombe underwent before he could bring himself to take part in this ceremony. The honours paid to Ralph were thought exaggerated even by the family, and it was not surprising that Dunscombe resented them as aimed maliciously at himself. He went to the station, however, in a mood which bears might contemplate with envy and despair to rival, leaving Hugh seated at the window of the Peele House.

From this elevation he presently observed Miss Palliser setting out alone for a walk; the day was tine, the house dull, Aunt Saxell in bad temper, and she herself particularly lively. Hugh descended the winding stair like an acrobat, and hurried in pursuit so fast that when Grace turned she said:

'Dear me, Mr. Acland, I thought it was a mad bull after me!'

'Only an idiotic calf, I assure you!' he answered, walking beside her.

'You are going my way?'

'Yes, if you don't mind.'

'On the contrary! I can put you down wherever you are going, and resume my course.'

'Miss Palliser, you encourage a very unfeeling class of wit. What have I done to be shot at continually in this way?'

'Do I shoot at you? It must be because you hit back so smartly. The dull Dales-women are not used to be caught up at a half-word, or a glance, or a tone!'

'The men round here must be a stupid lot, I see.'

'Indeed, you are quite mistaken!' Grace exclaimed warmly. 'For the county class they are just the same here as anywhere else, of course; but they've character, which Southerners haven't—generally. And as for the others, I can tell you that there's more intelligence and more fun in a cottage of our North-country than in a village of the Midlands, or a Parliamentary district in London.' Calming, she added, 'But we are not quick in the sense of smartness—I admit that.'

'Any facts you are good enough to impart, I treasure in my deepest soul,' Hugh answered, 'and especially if they concern your friends. I have now a much more exact conception of the Border character. But you failed to listen attentively.'

'You said the Dalesmen were a stupid lot!'

'Pardon me! My remark was that I now saw they must be a stupid lot, evidently referring to the context.'

'This sort of thing is quite in their way of humour——'

'Oh, indeed! Thank you, Miss Palliser'

'I didn't mean that! Their jests demand a lot of time and attention, that's all. I forget the context.'

'Please don't embarrass me with more explanation, then!—oh, must I? The cue was "caught up"—you said the Dalesmen were not quick at that exercise with you—and then I—this is torture, Miss Palliser!'

'So it is, poor boy, and I'm ashamed of myself. Thank you kindly all the same. Now I'll tell you something; I have heard from Miss Acland.'

In his utter surprise Hugh blurted out, after a thoughtless way he had, 'What on earth—er—I'm so awfully pleased, that I don't find pretty expressions! How did this delightful event come to pass?'

'Did not Mrs. Acland tell you that when Ave were in town—you don't for-get that time, perhaps?—she sent me a very kind message through Mr. Vane and aunt?

'Then this is what Mrs. Saxell referred to last night! My mother did not mention the incident; but she is always doing kind actions. It slipped her memory, no doubt—she has never seen you. I am overjoyed—well?'

'Well, auntie delivered the message, and after thinking about it for some days I made up my mind that I ought to reply, and I did. See, this was forwarded to me to-day from Scarsholme.'

Hugh read:

'MY DEAR MISS PALLISER,

'Mamma has instructed me to answer your graceful note. She congratulates herself upon the impulse that moved her to send you an expression of goodwill, and I am pleased to act as her secretary. It is agreeable to exchange messages of esteem during hostilities. Mamma is satisfied that Major Saxell is acting under an assurance of right, and she does not blame him; still less his mother, and still less again yourself. If we should ever meet, it will be with an expectation on my side that the acquaintance will be pleasing.

'Yours sincerely,

'EDITH ACLAND.'

'Isn't it just what such a letter should be under all the circumstances—so pretty, and nice, and cool?'

To Hugh, however, it suggested a good many reflections. Once again his mother had thought fit to take a step, without consulting him, without even mentioning the subject, that might well prove important and must certainly interest himself. This was irritating and alarming.

But, on the other hand, what a gracious step it was! By her delicate and becoming advances, Mrs. Acland had bridged the gulf which seemed to keep the families asunder. And the letter! Hugh could imagine the laughing diplomacy by which his sister had been coerced to write it, not unwilling. Grace would reply, no doubt, a correspondence would follow, and then—who could say what might happen! All this the doing of a mother whom he reproached with want of confidence! Hugh felt ashamed.

'Do you think,' Grace continued, 'that I might venture to write to Miss Acland direct?'

'Most certainly! Letters are written to be answered—especially by young ladies.'

'What a very cheap little witticism! If ever the records of primeval man turn up, I shall expect to see that sort of thing in his copybooks. Yes, I know you don't mean anything; but you should not get into the way of repeating commonplace without even the excuse of meaning it. Have you Miss Acland's photograph?'

Hugh took the locket off his chain and presented it; whilst Grace indulged raptures of admiration over the portrait of his sister, he devoured with his eyes the beauty not less exquisite, though less spiritual, which bent over the likeness. It did not offend him to be called 'boy,' nor to be patronized and schooled. Hugh's conceit was superior to that feeling. The memory of her engagement jarred upon him painfully from time to time; but, as Dunscombe said, India is a long way off, and a 'boy' may be capable of upsetting a boy-and-girl attachment. Hugh did not think of the treachery—would you have done so, reader, at his age? Would any man that ever lived outside the covers of a story-book?

'This is Mrs. Acland, I suppose?' Grace said, looking at the photograph opposite. 'I think you are the luckiest youth in the world to have such a mother and such a sister.'

'If I only get a wife to match—as beautiful as Edie, and as good, as bright, and high-spirited as my mother! I cannot be called a happy youth till then!'

'Surely you haven't thought of marrying yet?' she answered mischievously. 'That's quite a grave, grown-up amusement!'

'Grave amusement is a very happy expression. I have thought a good deal about it lately.'

Grace was evidently cogitating other matters.

'Tell me now/ she said, 'may I take Mrs. Acland's kind expressions sincerely— and Edie's too? I may call your sister "Edie"?'

'Yes, as a beginning!'

'Beginning of what?'

'Why, of friendship; what else? Presently it will be "darling" between you! Then you will kiss at brief intervals, and grow to one another like Siamese Twins. And all the young men of the neighbourhood will be attacked by jaundice, and fade in green despair.'

'Nothing fades green except old clothes; but all green things fade—leaves and eater-pillars and boys! You have not answered my question. Does Edie really and truly feel kind towards me? Would she like to be my friend? I have never had a friend except silly schoolgirls?'

'If Edie says so, it is true.'

'She doesn't say so! I want to ask her, and I daren't! "Will you? Say I am not wicked, nor stupid, nor vulgar, nor ugly, and I long to love her!'

'I will write this afternoon.'

'That's kind! What shall you say?'

'May I tell you?' he asked, warming suddenly.

'Please do!' But when Grace looked up in his face, she coloured, and added with a little smile, 'No! I'm sure you will put the request nicely, and that's enough.'

'I shall say, Miss Palliser——'

'You will say very pretty things, no doubt, which my modesty would be shocked to hear!'

'How do you know? I shall say——'

'I would rather not, really!'

'I shall say——'

'Don't tell me, I beg!'

When Miss Palliser was decided, a rare mood because she had rarely occasion, her manner forbade doubt. Hugh obeyed with some trepidation, but in two minutes they were chatting merrily again.

The party had returned when they got back, and Mrs. Ralph was holding a levee. Hugh retired to the Peele House, and wrote an enthusiastic letter, begging Edie to make definite overtures.

Next afternoon occurred the banquet, to be followed by a ball, or rather two balls, for the tenantry had their own. All the country-side, of every degree, accepted Lord Rainforth's invitation. As Dunscombe and Hugh sat in the Peele House, watching the line of carriages and gigs and tax-carts mounting the hill, the former muttered:

'How these creatures flock to the trough! In better days, nothing but an alarm of Scots on the Border would have called such a crowd to Daneham.'

The less important folk assembled in a large marquee, between the Hall and the 'Power, where public enthusiasm could not disturb the aristocrats. The host, his two sons, and all the guests bearing the name of Randall, sat out the early dinner of the tenantry, and made the usual speeches. They withdrew in time to dress for the fashionable entertainment, where the discourses went through a second edition. Dunscombe's handsome face was sullen as he heard the cheering for his younger brother. It was, in truth, an exaggerated welcome for a cadet who had done nothing since his birth to merit honour. People even asked in whispers what the demonstration signified.

Immediately after dinner, the aristocrats visited the marquee, now cleared. They danced a miscellaneous and amusing quadrille; then the ladies retired for their own ball. It is quite needless to tell how lovely Grace appeared in her robe of Indian muslin and blue silk. How and when it should be paid for was a question that did not cross her mind, though it qualified Mrs. Saxell's admiration. Hugh, of course, had secured as many dances as Miss Palliser's rather vague sense of etiquette allowed, to the disgust of other bachelors. Foremost among his rivals was a young Artillery officer on leave of absence from Meerut. He had served in the Afghan War, he knew X 3 Battery as well as his own, and Major Saxell was his most intimate friend, as he declared. Upon these credentials he claimed privilege in addressing Grace, and she granted it readily enough, until the young man had told all he knew about Dick. When he showed signs of exhaustion, and a wish to deviate from this topic, Miss Palliser did not pretend more interest.

Supper was announced for midnight, and Hugh had obtained the favour of escorting Grace. As the crowd pressed out of the ball-room, she said, 'I should so like another breath of air before going in!' and they strolled through an open window. The summer night was radiant, though the moon had almost set. Gaily talking they passed round the wing and gained the broad terrace at the back. Upon one side stood the tent, prettily warm with lights inside, and still resonant with music, though the guests had nearly all departed; solemn and still in front loomed the grey Peele House, its small lower windows faintly aglow with colour, those in the top story shining white in the moonbeams. Suddenly-interrupting herself, Grace exclaimed:

'Oh, Mr. Acland, now you can take me into the Tower without the knowledge of that disagreeable Lord Dunscombe! There is no one about!'

'Ask me anything else, but——'

'I ask you nothing but that! You won't? Then I shall go by myself! You are bold at following, I know!'

The taunt was successful. Hugh closed his arm on hers and led the way. 'You promised never to refer to that—that incident again!'

'Did I? Then it was on the understood condition that you never offended me again.'

'Your promises are not straightforward.'

'It depends. I should keep my word under proper conditions.'

'What are they?'

'It is not worth while to tell you. Do you know, Mr. Acland, you are not nearly so entertaining as you were at first!'

'I am not so light-hearted.'

'Then pray throw something overboard, and resume your buoyancy! What an odd, pretty, awful entrance! These are the only stairs? I feel as if I was going to execution!—oh, how charming—how!—what!——' and so on.

Grace was delighted with the hall and its plenishing. Hugh followed her about impatiently. Some of the younger guests had talked of dancing in the marquee, now almost empty, after supper, and the danger of discovery was imminent. But Grace would not listen to hints.

At length Hugh spoke out in despair. 'Don't play with that dagger, Miss Palliser! It is edged and poisoned as scandal!'

She understood his emphasis and his look; her animated complexion paled, her eyes dilated. 'Oh, how silly I am with all my cleverness! Let us go immediately! Why did you not tell me it was wrong?'

'I am afraid you would not have listened.'

'Perhaps not at first, but afterwards! Go on, and see if anyone's about.'

The terrace was vacant, but shadows swiftly turning chequered the canvas sides of the marquee. They slipped in unperceived, and Grace instantly recovered all her spirits. She called for a country-dance, and the ring of her happy laughter told that care was forgotten.

It was very late when Hugh sought the Tower, leaving broad day outside. Dunscombe was smoking moodily in a flare of candles. Pie had resisted with great effort the display of his ill-temper through the evening, but it now had full possession. At Hugh's entrance, however, he tried to be pleasant. They talked of Miss Palliser, and

Dunscombe renewed his warning.

'It's too late to advise me!' said Hugh.

'So bad as that already? No champagne in it? I hope the morning light will bring you clearness of vision.'

'The morning light was broad enough when I came in to show my fate.'

'Confound these summer mornings! One can turn gas off when it becomes too knowing. Well, you sympathize with me at last, Hugh, or you soon will, unless I am mistaken.'

'What do you mean?'

'What I have already hinted.'

'That she is a flirt? Excuse me, my dear Dunscombe, but the suspicion is preposterous.'

'Of course! But there is something else. Did you observe her with Henderson?—idiotic of me to ask! When he was talking of Meerut and Afghanistan and **chota hazari** and **pukarow** and all that, apropos of Major Saxell, the young lady looked as if she could have kissed his ugly face. It may have been acting, but I think not. If she's realty constant—that is, if she believes herself to be—so much the better for you. You're young enough to get over a broken heart before the shooting. By-the-bye, how old are you exactly?'

'Twenty-three last February. Why?'

'I was only wondering what was the difference between your age and Miss Acland's.'

'She is nineteen on December 10th.'

'What will your sister say when she hears you have deserted to the enemy?'

'Oh, she's half disarmed towards Miss Palliser. You know my mother sent a polite message, which Grace prettily acknowledged. Edie replied, of course, and a correspondence is about to begin. I think it such a charming incident!'

'You would, of course!'

'When a conversation runs into sneers, it's time to go to bed. Six o'clock, by Jove!'

'A pleasant hour! I promised to tell you the story of Pack Randall, and this is just the time. We'll turn in at seven precisely. In Pack's day, the brothers of our family were not so devotedly attached as they are now; I don't quite know when it was.

Pack, the eldest, had quarrelled with his father about politics, and with his brother Steeve about a young cousin who lived at Daneham, in the old Manor House, for the Castle was not built. The family took different sides, of course, in some trouble; and one day there was a skirmish, or a battle, or something. In the evening Pack came to this tower secretly, and he sent a message to his cousin begging her to come to him. She was not a prudent young person, and she did so. While they were talking, in this room, Steeve appeared, and with remarkable presence of mind drew his sword, stabbed Susan Randall to the heart, and charged at Pack. I don't know why he did so, but the historians of the time seemed to think such conduct quite natural; and I am not sure that they were wrong, in the abstract. Whilst Pack defended himself, Steeve dropped his sword suddenly, and fainted. You may imagine that the lady had Pack's first attention, and when he remembered his brother that individual was found to be dead. So, in process of time, was Susan. My excellent forefather was tried for murder; but it was proved that all Steeve's wounds had been caused by firearms, in the late engagement probably. So he got off; and in the final result, here I am. If Pack had been hanged, it is thought most probable that I should have been somebody else, and what a disaster for the nation that would have been! Rainforth did his best to get a conviction, however. We were a merry family in those days, and we keep the tradition so far as altered circumstances will allow.

'That is the reason why there are restrictions on the intercourse between the Castle and the Peele House. Now, we have three-quarters of an hour yet before surrendering. Let us discuss this story, and I'll tell you another.'

'Your legends and your temper are equally grim. I don't feel equal to discussion, even if I could keep awake.'

'Go to sleep in your chair, but don't leave me alone! Look! There's Steeve's sword, with the blood still upon it, they say. If I wasn't so confoundedly timid about hurting people's feelings I'd have the rusty old thing cleaned.' He approached the embrasure to take it. 'Why, here's Miss Palliser's bouquet! Oh, guileless youth, do you thus trifle with the love of the war-worn soldier, and go to bed with a smooth conscience? Here's a subject for discussion that will rouse you! Keep on reciting the circumstances until I implore you to go to bed!'

Hugh's face betrayed him. In a changed voice Dunscombe said:

'Miss Palliser has been here?'

Hugh could not find a word to urge.

'I would not, I could not have believed that you were capable of such a breach of hospitality.'

Hugh coloured with anger and shame, but sat speechless.

'You knew our rules, and you knew what we are. If my father learns this, the consequences will be most serious to me. It is shameful, Acland!'

'I have nothing to answer! Put my apology into the most abject words you please, but spare me your insults!'

'I have not insulted you.'

'No? Then I won't wait till you begin.'

Hugh took up his paletot and quietly went out into the joyous splendour of a summer morning.

CHAPTER VII.
MR. BEAVER.

MY DEAR HUGH,

'Don't be so confoundedly touchy. If I spoke harshly, make allowance for the surprise, and for family annoyances which have been upsetting me, as you know. I apologize most sincerely. Write by return of post, like a good fellow as you are, and say you know I am

'Always yours,

'DUNSCOMBE.

'Observe that this is written within ten minutes of your departure.'

General Randall indulged a lifelong practice of inspecting every department of a household in which he might chance to reside, that fell within male province. He also took brief and incidental but vigorous forays into the feminine realm; for a long presidency of regimental canteens had brought a miscellaneous store of domestic matters within his purview. On the morning after the ball he was up at his usual hour, and found a superb opportunity to examine the field-state and the general returns of Daneham. I can quite understand that an old soldier upon holiday may be detested by servants. He is restless, up at all hours, and if inclined to pry no penetralia are sacred. Then he knows so much, and he is so painfully direct in questioning. Woman's business is no mystery nor taboo for him. Dear old General Randall, who made no use at all of his discoveries, was dreaded like a plague at Daneham.

On this occasion he questioned and advised everyone about the place. And at noon, with Lord Rainforth's permission, he visited the Tower. Dunscombe was still in bed, but he would insist on seeing him.

'Are we summoned to chant a madrigal under Ralph's window?' his lordship asked, yawning.

'I have called upon a serious matter, Dunscombe. Do you know that young Acland brought Miss Palliser here last night?'

'Well?'

'Did you know?'

'You mean to ask, did the governor know? I presume you have seen him before coming here?'

'I mean nothing more than I say. Did you know?'

'I know that a breach of the family regulations was committed. Après?'

'I was not thinking of your father for the moment, but of the scandal. It makes a certain difference, of course, if you were informed of Miss Palliser's visit.'

'I didn't know she was under your charge, General. You have a serious responsibility, it strikes me.'

'Miss Palliser is not in my charge, but the honour of a, brave soldier absent on duty to his Sovereign is the care of any man worthy the name. I ask once more, did you know of this business?'

'I regret I'm too sleepy to answer. Would you kindly pull clown the blinds before you go?'

'No, I will not. Lord Dunscombe!' and the General stalked out.

No whisper of her foolish doings had reached the public ear when Grace came down to breakfast. She left with Mrs. Saxell immediately after, and among the gentlemen who thronged to say good-bye Grace smiled sarcastically to note Hugh's absence.

He meantime walked to Preston. The curious look of passers-by warned him that dress-clothes, buckled shoes, black silk stockings, and a white tie are unusual on a North-country road at seven a.m. Before reaching the town he had made up his mind to visit Wolfingham; the key of the mystery lay with Mr. Beaver, so Mrs. Acland thought. Hugh did not propose to call on him, of course. Such an idea could not enter his head after late experiences. But it might be desirable to know what the gentleman was doing. Any way, a run to "Wolfingham could do no harm, and he would have the melancholy satisfaction of beholding the scene of his father's death. They would not expect him home for some days.

So Hugh bought clothes at Preston, and in the evening he reached the village of Wolfingham, put up at the Royal Beaver, and invited the landlord to have a glass of wine after dining.

'An odd name you have chosen for your house,' he said, to begin conversation.

'Gentlemen mostly think it odd, but I didn't invent it, sir,' the landlord answered. 'All this county belongs to Mr. Beaver; and he says, leastwise his forefathers used to say, that the crown of England was theirs by right. So the inn here has been called "The Royal Beaver" time out of mind.'

'I am most agreeably surprised to find such comfortable quarters in a small village like this. It's quite a large hotel you've got, landlord, with stabling for a troop of cavalry, as it seems to me. And excellently managed, too! Where do you find your customers?'

'Ah, that's a story, sir. You see, when Mr. Beaver was a young man, he had a deal of company, more than his house could hold—ay, and more than this inn could hold, into the bargain. Besides the stabling you see, I've pulled down a matter of twenty boxes, with servants' rooms and all that.'

'Mr. Beaver hasn't much accommodation, I suppose?'

The landlord laughed with intense amusement. 'That's a good un sir!—you'll excuse me, but that *is* a good un, that is! Why, you might a'most put my house into the old hall at Beaverlowe, and the chimneys wouldn't touch the roof; and what they call the new hall is bigger than that. As for stables, lord bless you, sir, it's a cavalry barrack!'

'But I've heard Mr. Beaver doesn't entertain so much now?'

'That's where it is, and my house is empty in consequence. But I don't complain, sir. Though there's never a soul besides the neighbours comes nigh the place, it's kept up just as it always has been—equal to give a duke his supper and his bed, if one should come this way.'

'The house seems quite new.'

'My father built this one; but the name's been here, as they say, ever since the stream ran. Do you chance to know anything about our stream, sir?'

'I have very sad associations with it.'

'Excuse me, sir, but I was sure of that when I saw your face. Your name will be Acland? Ay, I remember you a baby, sir, and I could almost think I was a boy again myself, talking to your father. The likeness is extraordinary. And Mrs. Acland, sir? I hope the poor lady is well?'

'Very well. You remember my father's death?'

'As if it was yesterday! A sad circumstance, sir! They still talk about it in the village. He was riding our old horse, you know, which had crossed the ford a thousand times—aye, and more than that! How that horse came to miss the road none of us can make out.'

'But you don't doubt my father was drowned?'

'Ah no, poor gentleman! But it was an extraordinary thing. There's no doubt of his being drowned, is there, sir?'

'None at all. Is Mr. Beaver at his house now?'

'He never leaves it. Mr. Beaver did all his gadding when he was young. If you'd like to see the ford, I'll show you in the morning with pleasure—that is, I'll show you, sir.'

The landlord was called away, and Hugh found himself alone, with several hours to get through before bedtime. He tried to sit and think, a process that seems easy to dull mortals, easy also perhaps to philosophers and men of stupendous nature, but mighty difficult to persons of average intelligence. Giving up the effort, he rose and went down.

The passage was occupied by a number of men, and going out, Hugh was aware that they looked at him keenly, though with the side-glance of politeness. It occurred to his mind that if those fellows could be led to gossip, they might possibly give him useful information, and he re-turned shortly.

No bagmen visited this hamlet, and the landlord, with a rare intelligence, had refrained from entitling his parlour the commercial room. More than that, since farmers did assemble there pretty often, lie had painted 'Farmers' Room' upon the door. But the occupiers at that hour of the evening were not precisely agriculturists, though at such a place every inhabitant has an interest in the soil. Hugh thought to recognise such characters as a lawyer's and a parish clerk, a churchwarden, a schoolmaster, a doctor's assistant, a butcher, the keeper of the post-office, and so on—ten altogether. Most probably he quite mistook their avocations, but for convenience we may identify these worthy folk by the functions Hugh assigned them. Any way, he saw that all were residents, and all of an age to recollect his father's death.

The blank and sudden pause that followed his entrance told more plainly than words the subject of an animated conversation that had been proceeding. But in the remotest village nowadays some travelled person may be found who tries, at least, to cover an awkward incident like this. The lawyer's clerk said promptly, 'Good-evening, sir. I hope I see you well.' And the parish clerk added in emulation, 'I was just about to drink, sir, and I humbly put your health in it!'

The others muttered approval, and dipped their noses to the toast.

'I am obliged,' said Hugh, 'and I'll drink your healths heartily as soon as I can get the means. But I don't flatter myself that this kind reception is due to my own merits. You recognise me, and you are good enough to transfer to me the kindly feeling you had towards my father.'

This little speech produced an effect. The lawyer's clerk—a man of humour evidently—choked behind his hand; the) butcher flushed; the parish clerk blew out his cheeks; the churchwarden assumed an air of sternest scrutiny, as suspecting irreverent sarcasm; the schoolmaster looked as if he would like to get out of this:—in I short, each after his fashion plainly expressed his repudiation of the theory.

Hugh coloured with indignant embarrassment. 'You seem to have a less pleasant I recollection of my father,' he said, 'than I had hoped. I will not intrude upon you.'

'No indeed, sir!' exclaimed the lawyer's clerk. 'We only remembered that your father was a gentleman, and didn't mix with the like of us——'

'And the cockerel pipes as the old cock crows!' muttered the butcher.

'It isn't likely, sir, that Mr. Jones here, nor yet Mr. Brown, not to name the rest of us, would wish to hint anything unkind. Pray sit down, sir. We're heartily glad to see you!'

'That's what we are!' everyone protested, and truly enough, doubtless, for a sensation equal to this had not enlivened their village since the great event of 1862.

Hugh seated himself, after a moment's hesitation. 'Now, gentlemen,' said he, 'quite in a friendly way, among ourselves, what were your grievances against my father?'

They sat silent, not for want of matter evidently, but in embarrassment.

'Let it rest, sir/ said Mr. Brown at length. 'We all of us recollect you kindly. if you're the little chap Mr. Acland used to carry on his saddle. And we should like to hear how you've got on.'

'But I want to know. I want you to speak out, and I promise not to take offence. Did my father harm any of you, or yours?'

All said 'No,' but with a reluctant air.

'What do you mean?' cried Hugh, warming. 'Did he?'

'He ran over Johnny Tubbs in one of his fits!' muttered somebody.

'But the child was little hurt, for I attended him,' Mr. Brown answered. 'And Mr. Acland gave his father twenty pounds.'

'Well, is that all? Did he owe you any money?'

'That he did!—but we've been paid.'

'Then what is it?'

'You can see pretty well, sir,' said the doctor's assistant. 'Mr. Acland didn't give himself pains to make common people like him.'

'Common people?' murmured the churchwarden indignantly.

'You have desperately long memories here! I hope they're as good for cherishing kindnesses as for slights. When the offender was drowned at your doors, and near twenty years have passed, random conduct might be forgiven and forgotten!'

'But if it comes to that,' growled the butcher, 'was he drowned—eh, Mr. Williams?'

'What do you mean by that?' Hugh exclaimed again. 'Does anyone here doubt it?' He had identified Mr. Williams by the general glance turned on him; it was the schoolmaster.

'This isn't right, Mr. Grubb,' he cried, in vexation and alarm. 'I have never said it was Mr. Acland I met—never! I defy any gentleman here to charge me with it'

Hugh calmed at once. 'There is no question of charging you, Mr. Williams,' he said quietly. 'Pray let me hear what you fancied you saw.'

The schoolmaster was persuaded to tell his story at length: the facts were few enough, but circumstances and incidents and explanations made a long narrative of them. In the winter of 1862 he was suffering from sleeplessness and nerves, and he went to some friends at Laystone. On the night of December 9th he had not shut his eyes for a week or so; thinking that the open air might relieve him, he rose quietly and left the house. It was about two a.m., very dark and misty. Passing the post-office, where there was a lamp-post, he saw, to the best of his belief at the time, Mr. Acland, who dropped a letter in the box and walked on. It struck him as curious that a gentleman should be out at such a time, but much less extraordinary in the case of Mr. Acland than of any other person he ever heard tell of. On returning home Mr. Williams fell asleep, the first time, if you would believe his solemn word, etc. He slept and dozed all that day, and it was not till evening that they told him of the drowning. In the excitement of the moment he disputed it, telling what he thought he had seen. Of course it was fancy—no one could be so well convinced of that as himself. Mr. Williams appealed anxiously to his habitual audience to confirm the declaration that he had never pretended otherwise.

They all admitted the statement of fact, but with glances suggesting that they knew better than Mr. Williams himself what he had seen. The parish clerk whispered, as all rose upon the stroke of ten: 'It was your poor father's ghost, sir! He was not one to rest in his grave, and much more at the bottom of the river! Good-night, sir!'

Hugh begged Mr. Williams to stay, and he remained most unwillingly. No more information could he give. He had not observed Mr. Acland's dress, or anything about him. He did not believe that the figure was a ghost. The incident was a common case of mistake.

Hugh passed a wakeful night. The feeling of these honest villagers, who knew his father well, and remembered him bitterly, was distressing. That trouble he must keep to himself, but the story of Mr. Williams was no such simple question. Under the new circumstances, it had quite a new significance. Hugh had gone further than prudence advised in hinting to the schoolmaster that it was not thought impossible by some, the man he saw might have been Acland himself; but all the more earnestly Williams protested that his eyes had deceived him. Hugh could not doubt that he would declare the same in a court of justice, if called upon to tell his tale.

And so, after painful thought, he resolved to keep this secret also against his mother and all the world.

Under the landlord's guidance next day Hugh visited the melancholy spot. Scarcely twelve inches depth the water had that bright summer morning. Boys were playing there, laughing and calling to one another. A brood of ducks swam to and fro beneath the alders; cattle stood knee-deep in the river, whirling their tails restlessly.

'It doesn't seem the place for a strong man to drown,' said the landlord; 'but there's a power of water in flood-time. The horse landed there betwixt the alders.'

'Anyone standing on the bridge could see the whole breadth of the ford.'

He was thinking of Peake's statement.

'As for that, sir, it was near nine o'clock, and I was abroad myself that night. You couldn't see your hand before you.'

'Peake had a light, perhaps.'

'Not that I ever heard of. He heard a noise of splashing and shouting—that was all.'

'You forget. Peake saw my father washed under the bridge.'

'I don't remember that,' he continued dubiously; 'and I heard him tell the story above a time or two before he left these parts. No doubt you're right; but if he did, he must have carried a lantern.'

The landlord thought over this idea silently for awhile, as they turned back.

'Ah, well,' said he at length, 'it's a long while ago. You were speaking of Mr. Beaver yesterday, sir. He was in the house at that moment, drinking a glass of ale at the bar in his pleasant way.'

'Did you mention me?'

'I didn't, sir, because——' he hesitated.

'But some of them did.'

'You thought he might not care to hear my name?'

'Why not, sir?'

'You should know better than I.'

'Well, he might not, of course——I don't know anything about it. But, as I was saying, some of the men did name you. You're so like your father, you see, that all the village has been talking. When I came down from your room, sir, he spoke to me about you.'

'What did he say?' Hugh asked eagerly.

'He asked how you looked, and how Mrs. Acland was, and that. Always civil and good-hearted is Mr. Beaver, though people who don't know him don't like him, I dare say. Ten to one he will call to-night, coming from the cattle-show at Battley.'

Hugh had intended to leave in the afternoon, but nothing pressed, and the chance of seeing Mr. Beaver, perhaps of speaking to him without formality, made a strong temptation. He wrote to Mrs. Acland, and hung about the inn.

Late in the afternoon a gentleman rode up, two grooms behind him. The village women wreathed themselves in smiles; the grocer and the linendraper ran to their doors, and bowed and rubbed their hands with an expression of beatitude. No need to ask who the Squire is when be rides through his own hamlet. Hugh saw a slight, wiry man, who carried his years jauntily.

The face was very handsome, in a highbred style, but very keen; the smile ready to his thin lips had something sarcastic; but a pleasant-looking gentleman, and the greeting of the villagers seemed warm. Hugh observed nothing to justify his mother's strong expressions. Mr. Beaver's dress was not so quiet as it might have been. A. loose scarlet necktie, with a jewel in it that glitters superbly, is not the usual costume for elderly gentlemen who visit cattle-shows; and a pair of grooms, mounted on thorough-breds of pedigree, might be thought pretentious.

Mr. Beaver dismounted at the inn door, and Hugh went downstairs. Two or three farmers returning from market stood outside the bar, and with them Mr. Beaver had instantly begun a merry conversation. He looked up sharply as the youth went by, watched him lounge to the doorway, and then entered the bar. Presently a servant came to Hugh and asked him to step inside. He did so. Mr. Beaver was alone. He did not offer his hand, but began at once, standing—

'I should have known you, Mr. Acland, wherever we met. Many pleasant memories of mine are associated with your face, and some which I do not care to dwell on. I presume you have come here about a matter of which Mrs. Acland has twice written?'

'I had no fixed intention whatever in coming.'

'Well, I called this evening to see you. I can say to a son what I was embarrassed to write to a mother. Mrs. Acland seems to fancy that this Raikes, who claims to have been your father, was Harry Hardwicke—of that I know nothing, of course, one way or other. But Mrs. Acland thinks that I can tell something of Hardwicke. She is quite mistaken. The circumstances of his departure from Laystone are probably unknown to her. On that night, after Hugh Acland had dined with him, the Rector happened to call, and found Hardwicke drunk. He had at least more judgment than to apply to me after that disgrace.'

'I don't see why you should feel embarrassment in telling my mother this, sir. She wrote twice.'

'It is not that. If I took any part in this inquiry, I should be obliged to speak the truth. And that I am very unwilling to do.'

'It would be unpleasant for us?'

'It would. Acland told me that he meant to desert your mother.'

'When did he tell you this?'

'On the night he carried his resolve into effect,' Mr. Beaver answered, with a steady searching look.

'Will you speak frankly, Mr. Beaver?' said Hugh, after a pause.

'I will speak frankly, so far as I know. But in confidence.'

'Do you believe that Raikes was my father?'

'I supposed you were going to ask that, and I qualified my promise. Whether Raikes was Hugh Acland I cannot possibly say, but it does not seem to me improbable, and no one knew your father so well. This is in confidence; but you may tell your mother, with my kindly wishes, that if I have not answered her it is because I can do your cause no service. "When I can help her I certainly will.'

He motioned to go. They had not sat down, and both went out. As Hugh passed the bar window, he heard Mr. Beaver resume his laughing talk with the farmers.

Mrs. Acland did not get her son's letter in time to prevent grave anxiety. For Dunscombe's note, carried to Preston by a groom, travelled with Hugh to town, and was delivered the same night. His signature upon the envelope naturally perplexed the ladies. The morning post brought a second letter, bearing Lord Rainforth's autograph on the outside. And meantime arrived Hugh's servant, expecting to find his master at home. All he knew was that Moore, Lord Dunscombe's man, told him to pack and follow Mr. Acland, who had left. Seriously alarmed, Mrs. Acland telegraphed both to Rainforth and Dunscombe. The latter did not reply; the former answered:

'Lord Rainforth presents his compliments to Mrs. Acland, and desires to inform her that Mr. Hugh Acland was Lord Dunscombe's guest. Lord Rainforth is not ac-quainted with his movements.'

This harsh reply increased the consternation. Grave measures impended, when Dunscombe called with the telegram, which had been redirected to him in town. He admitted that Hugh left unexpectedly, and his embarrassment suggested all kinds of suspicion. If all was right why did he not explain? Dunscombe took himself away precipitately, and forthwith Mrs. Acland opened Lord Rainforth's letter:

'SIR,

'I understand by common report that last evening you escorted a young-lady through the Peele Tower, without asking my consent, nor, I believe, my son's. You may be ignorant of the laws of propriety, or indifferent to them; but on arrival here you were made acquainted with the customs respected in a family that had received you with kindness. I trust myself to say no more.

'Your obedient servant.

'RAINFORTH.'

They sat aghast.

'It was Miss Palliser! Oh, these people are our Fates, mamma!' Edie cried. 'And I was beginning almost to like her. Let us read Lord Dunscombe's letter!'

That relieved them somewhat. Hugh was not lying in Daneham woods with a bullet through him. And next day came his letter from Wolfingham, which they read together.

'The landlord forgets that Peake had a lantern,' said Mrs. Acland. 'He was a cow doctor, and had been visiting a farm in the neighbourhood.'

'I wish Hugh would rest quiet, and leave things to wiser heads!'

'He acts according to his nature, my dear, and we have no cause to complain of that upon the whole. There are few boys of high spirit and quick temper who have given their friends so little annoyance. I think we need not speak to Hugh about Lord Rain-forth's letter. I will put it on his table.'

'He has done nothing wrong, mamma, I'm sure of that; but he's so very thought-less sometimes. And the dear, silly fellow seems to have found a kindred spirit.

Don't you begin to think, mamma, that Hugh's admiration for Miss Palliser is becoming rather grave?'

'I have no secrets from my children, dear. The idea struck me long ago.'

'And in the same breath you declare that you have no secrets!'

'***Distinguons,*** my child! I did not say that I have no thoughts which I keep to myself. Life would be intolerable if we told all that passes through our minds. Many ideas occur to me which you would not like to hear.'

'I don't believe it! Try me!'

'As a mere idea, I could wish you were married to this man or that whom I dare not suggest.'

'You unnatural mother!' cried Edie, blushing.

'You see! It does not answer even to hint all one thinks!'

'Name one man in particular.'

'No, we have gone quite far enough. Let us return to Miss Palliser.'

'I believe, mamma—I have always suspected—that you would like to see me engaged to Lord Dunscombe!'

'Then you yourself do not confide every thought to me?'

'You do not deny it?'

'I cannot control your wild ideas. But, to speak seriously, since you have introduced the subject, you know I would not interfere with your choice. I have the most perfect confidence in my daughter's judgment. But there are few men or women who secure the grand prize.'

'I understand what you mean. But, indeed, I don't ask for so much.'

'Only all the virtues combined with all the graces! Sad experience has taught me to understand men! You would not accept a Christian hero if he presented himself—not one, at least, of the type generally understood. Don't stare! I will explain. You demand, before choosing, certain qualities which are not correlative, as the word goes, with others that you exact—that is to say, I never met them together.'

'Explain the explanation, dear.'

'It is difficult—hardly possible, perhaps, for your inexperienced comprehension. You demand a handsome man. Oh, not the tailor's type—much less the hairdresser's; but one a good deal more difficult to find. Then the hero must be bright and quick, but at the same time firm; enterprising, yet gentle; self-confident and modest; brilliant and clever, but pious; a very fascinating creature, and not too young, but never in love till he saw you. Such a being may exist, for the possibilities of human nature are endless; but, so far as I have had opportunities to judge, half the qualities you ask are not to be reconciled with the other half. Now, Lord Dunscombe has merits, but he is very human.'

'I should not be afraid, so far as that goes, to take him with his faults, if I loved him. My self-conceit goes as far as that, for I quite admit that he has merits, and I believe he is fond of me. But who could love a man who cannot go straight by his own will? You do not wish me to marry him?'

'That is going much too far. I see you have thought about it, and that's enough; I mean, that you have considered the matter. Let us return to Miss Palliser. Have you kept her letters?'

'Yes, they're so odd!'

She read them aloud, with judicial deliberation. How astonished would Grace have been to hear the sentences, put down as fast as heedless pen would follow eager brain, thus weighed and analyzed.

'What is your opinion, mamma?'

'I should think her what they call a smart girl—that is, quick, thoughtless, worldly, amiable enough, good-tempered, particularly well aware of her fascinations. Not at all an unprofitable friend for my brooding little daughter if circumstances permitted; and, I must say, not an impossible sort of bride for my son. I should not be inclined to condemn her unheard. Hugh might fall into hands very much worse.'

'I am not sure about that, but I should have liked to know her. Of course, it is impossible now!'

'Why, darling? We know that they have acted very foolishly, and we are not surprised. To desert Miss Palliser would be a kind of admission that they were worse than foolish. Do not drop your correspondence. I am afraid the poor girl will suffer for her imprudence, and a letter from you would be a comfort.'

'How kind and thoughtful you always are! But really, when Hugh is in love with her, is it judicious?'

'It just occurs to me that we are talking foolishness indeed! Miss Palliser is engaged to Major Saxell. Mr. Vane told me so. Probably Hugh is not aware of that.'

'Engaged? Then she is no friend for me, mamma. That settles the question.'

'I don't see how, my dear. If she has been 'flirting with Hugh, that is another matter. But engagement does not cure silly girls of their silliness, unfortunately. Wait at least until your brother comes.'

'I will if I can. You are quite too calmly good-natured, mamma.'

When Hugh reached home, very late in the evening, his elaborate explanations of the sudden departure from Daneham were cheerfully admitted, and he thought himself vastly clever. But this pleasing sensation was dispelled at sight of the letters on his dressing-table. He answered Lord Rainforth at once:

'MY LORD,

'For the offence I gave without premeditation I apologize. I venture to think that it did not justify the words addressed to me, but if they afford your lordship relief I must not complain. Lord Dunscombe knew nothing of the matter, and when he heard, he expressed sentiments so nearly akin to your lordship's that I left his roof then and there.'

To answer Dunscombe was not so easy, and whilst Hugh meditated Mrs. Acland tapped at his door, in the prettiest of caps and the freshest of peignoirs.

'Now, dear,' she said, 'tell me all about it'

'About what, mams, for gracious' sake?'

'Oh, about one matter I can guess as much as is necessary. You have been to Wolfingham? What happened there?'

Hugh told his meeting with Beaver, and gave the message. Mrs. Acland listened thoughtfully.

'So that is what has changed you?' she said. 'Oh, don't trouble to deny it, my boy. Beaver is still my enemy? Well, the right will triumph at last, but it's cruel to make a son distrust his mother.'

'I distrust you!' he cried, with a growing emphasis on every word. 'Not if all the Beavers were translated, and spoke with the tongues of angels! But I begin to think, dear, that we may have been mistaken.'

'And I tell you we are not, Hugh!' Mrs. Acland exclaimed, with sudden vehemence. 'That falsest and most cunning of villains has succeeded so far! He has made you doubt, and that was all he dared at present. But we may look for more developments of his ingenuity!'

'We can so easily disconcert him, mother, with a bold resolution.'

'By admitting that Hardwicke was Hugh Acland—by allowing their hate to beat us at last? Never! I would rather die here, now, than give them such delight! But I am very wrong to show temper! We will talk pleasantly and gravely. You propose to give up your property because Mr. Beaver does what he can to support Mr. Hardwicke's imposture?'

'It will not be our fortune, mother. We shall still be rich. And the fact that Peake is evidently exaggerating had more weight than anything Beaver said.'

'I forgot that. Peake carried a lantern, and he always said so.'

'That, if proved, would change the case entirely! It is stated in his first deposition?'

'No doubt. I have the local newspapers, which referred to the accident. There you will find it. Is that all?'

'That is quite all.' He had made up his mind to keep silence about the ghost "Williams had seen, and his mother's heat confirmed the resolve. But that heat bewildered him. Hardwicke's jealous disappointment flaring up in death might, in a sense, be understood; but why was Beaver supposed to be implacable? What grievance had he? And why did Mrs. Acland, so calm and easy-going and reasonable, flash with anger at his name?

If her keen eyes observed Hugh's indecision, she did not remark upon it. 'Will you be satisfied now, Hugh,' she said, 'and leave all the matter to me? Twice you have interfered in a delicate and painful inquiry—how many more times I do not know. But on both these occasions grave disputes have arisen between us. If your confidence in me is restored, promise that henceforth you will let your mother conduct the affair.'

'I promise faithfully,' Hugh exclaimed, not without relief.

'I register that vow, and we will talk of pleasant matters—Miss Palliser, for instance?'

'I am in love, mams, and she and I have got into a scrape.'

'Are you certain the young lady is free?'

'You have heard something, then? It is absurd to suppose that there can be a serious engagement between Grace and Major Saxell, when they have not met since she was a child.'

'Before I decide about that, tell me what has passed.'

'I recognise your quiet sarcasm there, mams. If Miss Palliser is so fast now, she may have been precocious enough to fall seriously in love at ten years old! But, indeed, she is unlike other girls.'

'As the mother of a girl, I cannot pretend to regret the difference excessively. But let me have her story, which will not be put in the worst light by you, I conclude.'

'It is not quite a laughing matter, I fear!' said Hugh.

To own one's self wrong is pleasanter than to own one's self weak. He accepted so much more of the responsibility for a joint escapade than belonged to him, that the account might easily have been understood in a sense very different to the truth. But Mrs. Acland was not deceived.

'You do not use the privileges of your sex,' she said, with smiling bitterness. 'The world will be quite ready to throw all the blame on Miss Palliser!'

'Poor child! Yes, I have been thinking of that. Couldn't you write to her kindly?'

'I'm afraid,' she said, 'that would be rather injudicious and scarcely dignified.'

'Well, Edie might! They have been corresponding, and she owes Miss Palliser a letter, I think.'

'You are aware of that?'

'Of course! There was no harm in her showing it me, was there?'

'There is no harm, I hope, in anything my son allows. It may be difficult to persuade Edie, however.'

'Oh, I think she would give her life for you, mams, and almost for me. She puts little value on it herself, poor dear! I can persuade Edie.'

'Well, I have no objection. Suppose you sketch your idea of the letter which would comfort Grace.'

Hugh wrote a draft, not without hesitation, nor abundance of erasures, When it was presented Mrs. Acland laughed.

'Why, what is this? So far as I can understand plain English at a late hour of the night, it is a warm invitation to take refuge in Eaton Square if things turn out uncomfortable at home! Edie will never transcribe this, Hugh, and I should not allow her! Let us dismiss the subject for a while. In the morning I will try my own ability.

Now, have you answered Lord Rainforth?'

Hugh showed the letter.

'It is very well,' said Mrs. Acland. 'I should add the expression of a hope that Lord Rainforth will accept the apology on his son's account. Put that in a form as dignified as you please!'

'It is all owing to their silly, musty practices at Daneham! You are very anxious, mams, to exculpate Dunscombe with his father.'

'One of my chief employments lately has been to undo the mischief my boy has wrought. Have you answered Lord Dunscombe?'

'I think I shall not answer at all. To tell the truth, this affair comes in very timely to relieve me from an embarrassing position. Dunscombe has fallen into a habit of making me the confidant of his feelings towards Edie, though I have never encouraged him. It is a good opportunity to break off.'

'I do not encourage him myself. But you are well aware, Hugh, that I should be pleased to see Edie regard him with more favour.'

'Oh, mother, you don't know——'

'I know more, perhaps, than you! Lord Dunscombe is not an ideal husband. But his faults are not vices, and they would vanish for ever if he had a wife whom he loved and respected, as he does Edie. I should not hesitate to trust my child to him. Put romantic notions aside, Hugh, and compare Lord Dunscombe with other young men who would stand a chance of acceptance from her. She will marry neither a prig nor a rake, neither an outsider, nor a commonplace man, nor a vulgarian, nor a Philistine, nor an æsthete. The range of choice is very limited, for Edie is not even indifferent to good looks, and the youth whom I should call average horrifies her. Can you name one among those likely—that is, not wholly unlikely—to succeed in the long-run, against whom there are not arguments as strong as against Dunscombe, while the advantages, of any sort, are not incomparably less? Look at it in that way.'

'I can't, mams! It is not that Dunscombe is conspicuously fast as men go, but that he is so fast whilst declaring and protesting himself in love with Edie. If regard for her is not able to keep him straight now, when he has all to lose, how can you hope that it will be strong enough when he has secured her?'

'The argument is good as an exercise, but it is not borne out by experience of men. Dunscombe is one of those who could reform without an effort, if summoned, but do not trouble to resist temptation day by day with no distinct purpose before them. I know what you are going to say, but remember that I proposed to drop romantic ideas. However, this talk is all in the air. I shall not interfere with Edie by even a hint. What I ask of you is to accept Lord Dunscombe's apology, and resume, in appearance at least, your old friendship.'

'Well, I obey. But you do not expect me to be cordial? I will meet Dunscombe courteously, but I'll see no more of him than I can help.'

So that was decided. Hugh wrote a cold letter of forgiveness, and went to bed.

At the very earliest hour next day he waited on his mother, claiming her promise to draft the comforting missive for Grace, which Edie was to transcribe. It was drawn up, not without laughing but eager-disputes; and then came the greater difficulty. His sister refused downright at first, but gradually yielded to Hugh's coaxing and Mrs. Acland's light-hearted way of putting the matter. But she would take no suggestions, and wrote in her own style:

'MY DEAR MISS PALLISER,

'My brother has returned, and he has given us your nice messages. After hearing from Hugh all that passed, mamma desires me to say that she still desires to make your acquaintance when Mrs. Saxell can spare you.

'In haste/

'Do cross out "still," darling, and make it a little longer and a good deal more cordial. Say that you share the mams' wish, and end "affectionately," or "very truly," at least. You are not " in haste," and why say so to minimize the kindly effect?'

'I won't write in any other form, Hugh,' she answered, and signed her name 'sincerely.'

'I will try to believe all you say about Miss Palliser. If circumstances had been different I dare say I should have liked her. But as it is, I don't care to see her more than any of the rest.'

Later in the day Hugh asked for the newspaper paragraphs to which his mother had referred. They were very vague, mere rumours of a 'supposed accident at Wolfing-ham/ with no mention of Peake's name; only the report that 'a man crossing the bridge is said to have witnessed it.' Nothing about a lantern. But Hugh did not care to point this out.

CHAPTER VIII.
THE CONSEQUENCES.

GRACE PALLISER had known few troubles in life, and her facile disposition had easily shirked those which befell her. Sulks, and even tears, were not unknown in Mrs. Saxell's household, but only surface-deep. It was not temper, however, nor calculation, nor mischief, nor a bored craving for excitement which melted the young lady one day, a week after the ball. And with no faltering severity her aunt observed the deluge. She was as stern as she looked.

'I cannot now pretend to blame those people who have slighted you. Lady Rainforth's reply to my demand for an explanation is not at all unkindly under the circumstances. You have actually no excuse! Mr. Acland is a mere boy, and, I believe, a boy of fairly good principles. It was not to be expected that he would refuse when you pressed him, being a stranger to the usages of Daneham; but your conduct showed the extremest impropriety! And I have to say *that* of the girl on whom my son has bestowed all his gallant heart!'

'Oh, don't tell Dick!' Grace sobbed.

'I dare not keep the secret. You know too well that the country-side is talking, and scandal would carry it if I were silent!'

'He would not believe anyone else! Dick is so good.'

'The more reason I should tell him the truth.'

'Oh, aunt, I implore you! I will write—you shall see the letter.'

'I have decided which is the path of duty.'

Angry resolution shone in Grace's eyes also, tear-swollen though they were, when she looked up.

'You know, aunt, that Dick will never forgive me, if you repeat what those people are saying. But I hope and I think he will not forgive you either. I shall not bear all the blame.'

She left Mrs. Saxell glowering and speechless. The old lady was outraged in every feeling, but prudence warned her that the hint was not injudicious. A charge against Grace might finally bring about disagreeable consequences. Her sense of duty changed, and she waited only for some pretext to yield in a manner dignified and creditable.

But Grace never thought of trying former arts. She began a confession to Dick, and to her thus engaged Edie's letter was brought. Grace hardly read it before dashing off an answer:

'I was at my wits' end with penitence and bewilderment a moment ago! You are too tender-hearted to say what you do not mean, and I accept, oh, so thankfully! Mrs. Saxell can spare me now. May I come at once? Please, dear Miss Acland, remember how anxiously I shall expect your reply!'

In due course it arrived—from Mrs. Acland:

'It is not my habit to say more than I mean. Your visit would be gratifying to me, but I must tell you that we are going abroad immediately after the season. If that should not deter you I will write to Mrs. Saxell.'

'She will never accept that cold-blooded invitation,' said Hugh dolefully.

'My belief is,' Edie answered, 'seeing how Miss Palliser took my note, that this cold-blooded invitation of mamma's will bring her by next train!'

And the guess was not far wrong. Grace could not flatter herself that the Acland ladies were burning to make her acquaintance, but she made the best of it, wrote an acceptance with gratitude, and waited curiously rather than anxiously to see how her aunt took the business.

Mrs. Saxell glared over a letter which came two days afterwards.

'What is this madness? "What on earth does the woman mean?'

'Mrs. Acland asks me to stay with her until she goes abroad, and I accept!'

'You shall not go!'

'I will!' Their eyes met, and it was not Grace who faltered.

'I cannot believe you serious. To visit Mrs. Acland after what has passed would be another scandal, and a worse!'

'I know nobody else who would have me. We haven't any friends, aunt!'

'You do not deserve friends!'

'If so, it is unkind of yours to visit my faults on you.'

'Why do you want to go away?'

'Oh!'

There was length and depth enough in that ejaculation to supply a whole paragraph of answer.

'I have not written to Dick,' said Mrs. Saxell feebly.

'I have!'

'The long and the short of it is that you shall not quit my roof, if I have to use force to prevent you.'

'Don't be silly, aunt.'

With this astounding observation Grace left the room—and nature was not convulsed.

She wrote presently, announcing her arrival within three days. And then she became very busy, running in and out of the house. And so it chanced that the gardener's boy, carrying a letter to the post, was met by Grace, who relieved him of the duty, and forgot to fulfil it until the eve of her departure.

It is needless to describe the phases of a domestic struggle which ended, of course, in victory for the more reckless combatant. The power of the purse was all that Mrs. Saxell could count on practically, and that failed her. Grace had enough for the journey. She did not look beyond. Her aunt, or her guardian, or somebody, would supply the needful, of course.

Mrs. Saxell was not waiting in the breakfast-room as usual on the last morning, and after half an hour she did not appear. Grace actually brimmed with affection that day. She said to herself that to leave without good-bye would be agonizing, and so ran upstairs.

'Oh, please, please, dear!' tapping at the door—' a kiss and a kind word, please!'

The pretty coaxing tone was too much for Mrs. Saxell's sternness. She thought the rebel had given way, and opened her door, submitting to impetuous caresses. But in the midst thereof, Grace exclaimed:

'There's Giles's dogcart, auntie. It's such a relief to part affectionately.'

Mrs. Saxell pushed the girl away.

'You are a heartless, hypocritical creature! Stay with those people—they're of your own sort. Don't return here'

'Oh, darling auntie, don't begin again! Good-bye.'

The announcement of Grace's arrival caused a sensation, rather stupefying for the moment, in Eaton Square. Even Hugh stared before he sprang up and kissed his mother. Edie said, with colour heightened:

'I have accepted all you told us, Hugh, about Miss Palliser's innocence and impetuosity and the rest, but this is really indelicate. I cannot believe, until I have seen her, that any girl in possession of her senses could be so thoughtless. The best I can say for Miss Palliser is crushing to your hopes, Hughie.'

'How?'

'If she felt the very smallest interest in you, she would certainly not run away to your mother's house after what has passed.'

Hugh saw it, and his face lengthened, but he made an effort to defend the young lady.

'Then where is the indelicacy?'

'In forcing herself upon us. I never dreamed that the invitation would be taken seriously. Did you, mamma?'

'I hoped to have heard from Mrs. Saxell, certainly. But Ave must make her welcome now.'

'She will make herself welcome, mams!'

'Just so,' said Edie, 'and I shall bear the brunt. Mamma can escape her at any time.'

'Escape her!'

'And you, of course, will only meet her on show. All the penalty falls on me, who must be friendly and gossipy day and night! I detest her!'

'My darling princess! There are forms of blasphemy which rouse pity, not anger. I shall ask your revised opinion this day week.'

Then came Mrs. Saxell's letter:

'MADAM,—I am used to speak frankly. Your invitation to Miss Palliser is an impertinence. What your motive may be I do not try to guess. If you are not aware that she is engaged to my son, I give you the information. She has something less than £5,000 for her fortune. It would be superfluous, probably, to add that I cannot allow her to accept your kind invitation.'

'I'm glad you asked her now, mamma,' said Edie quietly. 'This explains a great deal.'

'You are a little angel!' her brother rapturously exclaimed.

Miss Palliser arrived in due time. Hugh was embarrassed, Edie grave, Mrs.

Acland cordial but restrained. Grace, alone, was perfectly at ease—used to admiration and liking from all she met, of high courage, thoughtless as a kitten, she did not know what shyness is. When Hugh introduced his sister, Grace blushed beautifully, and her eyes widened with pleased surprise.

'How could you utter such a calumny, Mr. Acland!' she said.

'What calumny?'

'To say that I —never mind! Would you kindly see about my boxes?—I am glad I did not know you, Miss Acland, before I invited myself so impudently. I should not have dared.'

'Am I so formidable?'

'Not formidable—at least—will you ever let me kiss you?'

'Whenever you please,' Edie answered, smiling, but unenthusiastic.

'I will try hard to deserve it! When I do, will you tell me? How stupid brothers are! Mr. Acland said we should run into each other's arms, and grow together, like Siamese twins! Oh, thank you! yes, the boxes are all right.'

I have no time to detail the course of little events which brought the girls to intimacy within a few days, admiring on both sides, protesting on Grace's part, kindly tolerant on Edie's. At the end of a week, the latter gave her opinion shortly.

'She is beautiful as a dryad! If Grace possessed a soul, she would be the dearest, brightest girl alive. Until she finds one, if

ever, she is not responsible.

'Can you help her, dear ?' asked Mrs. Acland.

'It's one of those cases, I think, mamma, where a woman's powers of magic are very limited; and I'm afraid Hugh would not be more successful even if he had a clear course.'

'Does she speak of her engagement?'

'Certainly. One can see that Grace regards it as a settled thing, and she has evidently a very great affection for Major Saxell. Whether she loves him in the way a girl should love her husband is another question.'

'If she did, I suppose that she would have what you call a soul?'

'Of course, if it were real love. But Grace's affection is quite a sisterly affair, and marriage seems to mean nothing besides freedom and fun and every sort of amusement that money brings. At the same time, she has it firmly fixed in her mind that

Major Saxell is very poor.'

'And does not try to reconcile the ideas ? That is carrying thoughtlessness to the verge of stupidity, and Grace is not stupid. Doesn't it occur to you that she may be reckoning on Major Saxell's success in his claim?'

'Oh, mamma! The girl is as honest and loyal as possible! She could not think of that when living with us.'

'I don't really believe she does. A curious character.'

'One thing is quite certain. Hugh is falling deeper and deeper in love with her, and he is quite capable of a serious passion. Are you not anxious, mamma?'

'Not very, dear. He will not break his heart. Lovely as Grace is, and gifted with more attractions than we women can appreciate, she is not the girl for whom men suffer lifelong agonies. I should think that Hugh will get over his disappointment in a few weeks, but I hope not.'

'I know you are as wise as affectionate. But why do you hope not ?'

'Because I think that he is going through an invaluable education. Hugh is very young in character, but headstrong, suspicious rather, and jealous of direction. If there were the slightest chance of his marrying Miss Palliser, I would do my utmost to stop it. for she has very much of his own disposition, and before they reached the altar they would have laid the foundation of a hundred quarrels, misunderstandings, tiffs, which might become serious afterwards. When both are older, and have had experience, they would be not ill-matched. The very best experience for Hugh will be this disappointment, not too painful.'

'I am sure you are right, if only it prove to be not too painful ! And meantime, mamma, there is a consideration which, perhaps, you have not thought of.'

'What is that ?'

'Hugh has quite ceased to trouble himself about the claim! He has not even talked of it for a week.'

'I did not consider that, you shrewd child! But it is very true. We have not had any alarms or excursions lately.'

'And my clever mamma had not observed that, until her silly daughter pointed it out! You don't do me the injustice—oh dear, how ought I to put it? You don't do me the injustice to suppose that I do not do you more justice than that ? That isn't neatly expressed. What I mean is, that I could almost believe you had foreseen the course things have taken since Hugh began to hope that Miss Palliser would come here, and had arranged accordingly—there!'

'All the suspicious nature of my offspring is not concentrated in Hugh, I see,' said Mrs. Acland pleasantly. 'But my plots are very harmless!'

'Don't I know that, kindest and best of mothers? If only Hugh's passion is as light as we trust it is!'

Grace was as happy as the day is long, counting it at the full twenty-four hours. The season died in a crush of gaiety. Mrs. Acland took the girls out a good deal, and a score of eligible chaperons were delighted to replace her at need. Opportunities of distinction in society are few, and the fame of a lady who had charge of two girls so notably beautiful was made for the night, possibly even for the morrow.

They very often met Lord Dunscombe, and he called in Eaton Square quite as frequently as the laws of decorum admitted. Grace soon got over the embarrassment of meeting him, for he laughed at her outrage on the Rainforth traditions. She observed, however, that Dunscombe and Hugh were not as friendly as they used to be, and boldly asked of the former if she was in any way the cause.

'So far from that,' he answered, 'no one is as well qualified as yourself to restore our understanding.'

'Then the quarrel must have been about me ? I am very clever in setting people by the ears, but not in smoothing them over afterwards. What shall I do?'

'Persuade Hugh to forgive me heartily. I behaved like a ruffian to him once.'

'Won't Edie or Mrs. Acland mediate ?'

'I could not ask them, and I implore you not to do so.'

'It is my duty, I suppose,' she said, and promised.

But the opportunity did not come. With all her carelessness, the girl felt this task awkward, and time went by. It became necessary to consider what she would do when Mrs. Acland and Edie went abroad. Grace took it for granted that the only course for her was a return to Scarsholme, and she did not repress her droll lamentations. Edie said one day, 'Do you think, mamma, that Grace means to hint that she would like to go with us to Italy ?'

'I'm quite sure she does not.'

'And so am I. So let us ask her.'

'I did not like to suggest it, but you really want a companion now. I shall be very busy and preoccupied until this affair of Major Saxell's is finished.'

'And then you know, dear, Hugh is not going with us. He would hardly have kept away from Scarsholme when he recollected that Grace was sitting there in tears and dishevelment longing for a comforter.'

'Do not put your cunning schemes to my account,' said Mrs. Acland, laughing.

So it was decided, and Miss Palliser lost her ill-regulated senses with joy and surprise. Mrs. Saxell wrote that if she delayed returning any longer, she need not take the trouble to return at all; but Grace only laughed, and said nothing to her host.

Riding up Grosvenor Place one day with Hugh, they met Lady Rainforth and Madge, who bowed distantly.

'I don't think I deserve to be treated so!' said Grace meekly, though her colour heightened.

'Don't regard those people! They are animated mummies, with a modern coat of paint.'

Grace laughed. 'But we were both. wrong, Mr. Acland! I own it, and I submit to the penalty. So should you!'

'I will submit to anything in your company.'

'Then make it up with Lord Dunscombe. He is so anxious to be friends!'

'I have no ill-feeling towards him. Let us talk of something else. When you are leaving in a few hours we might find a topic more interesting than Lord Dunscombe.'

'But I must have this off my mind!' Her beautiful eyes pleaded earnestly.

'Say "Forgive him for my sake," and I will love him.'

'I must not say that, Mr. Acland!'

'But that is what you mean? And why should you not say it ?'

'Frankly, I don't know why not. I will ask Edie.'

'Oh, Edie will give you reasons enough. If you feel, you must have an impression at least.'

'Hardly. Perhaps a girl is not right in asking personal favours.'

'That would depend,' he answered, pressing his horse closer; they had reached Rotten Row, and the crowd encompassed them. 'If Edie thought you'd ever consent to be her sister she would approve anything you did.'

'That I don't believe, Mr. Acland! Under the circumstances you funnily suggest, Edie would regard me and all my doings with the extremest disapproval.'

'She knows that I love you, and that would be enough for her if she did not love you herself.'

'Pray be more careful, Mr. Acland. Some one will overhear us, and may misunderstand.'

'They could not, for I am speaking quite plainly. I ask you to be my wife, Grace!'

'Your——But you know I am engaged?'

'There cannot be love between two persons who do not know each other by sight——'

'Why not as well as between two persons who don't know much of each other except by sight?'

'Then you don't love me ?'

'Oh, what an unfortunate girl I am!'

'Misery is very tolerable when other people bear all the sting of it! You cannot have been ignorant that I adored you from the first moment, and you have been playing with me!'

'I have not, indeed. Until this very instant, I never thought of you but as a kind, light-hearted friend.'

'Can you think of me gravely now ?'

'Yes—sadly! If I was to blame, I beg you to forgive me!'

'I am not quick at forgiving, you know. If you possessed the common feelings of womankind you could not have deceived me in this manner!'

Grace answered mildly:

'I sometimes think I haven't! But I am woman enough to regret this misunderstanding, bitterly!'

The real thought in her mind could not be expressed. It was astonishment at his presumption. Other young men admired her; all did, in fact. But she could not marry all, and she felt no inclination to make a choice. She liked Mr. Acland certainly, as she liked others who were bright and generous and warm-hearted and amusing. Why should he single himself out among the human race as destined for the prize? Grace did not feel complimented, but vexed and indignant.'

Perhaps Hugh saw the truth.

'You don't regret it,' he said roughly, 'for you don't comprehend it.'

They rode home silently. Mrs. Acland came to Hugh in his dressing-room.

'I have news that will relieve your mind, my son. Mr. Vane has written Major Saxell, advising him to drop his claim.'

'Oh, mother, I am so glad ! Then he is satisfied ?'

'Yes,' Mrs. Acland answered, smiling.

'As a cool, disinterested lawyer, Mr. 'Vane accepts evidence which does not convince my son——'

'Mother!'

'It is not your fault, dear! You have tried hard, I know, but I see you cannot believe—something, perhaps, you have heard which has not been trusted to me. I cannot tell that; but I can read your face. No, dear, darling Hugh, don't try to explain, since things have turned out so. The crisis is over. We will be quite happy and confidential again. Now, let us go to lunch.'

Grace had not learned, probably she would never learn, to hide a real feeling, and Hugh did not attempt it. Within three minutes Mrs. Acland and Edie knew as well as if they had overheard that those two had had an unsatisfactory explanation. And so they exerted themselves to make talk. After lunch the brother and sister remained alone. They congratulated one another on the issue of the question so far.

'Now,' said Hugh, 'I can start on my travels.'

'Where do you think of going ?' Edie asked, without surprise or alarm.

'Anywhere, so long as there's big game and savages in the neighbourhood.'

'You don't really mean that ? Oh, Hugh, she is not worth your honest heart nor our tears.'

'I know her better than you, and I can't help it. I must get away, darling ! Help me to persuade my mother.'

'If it is so, I will help you ! My poor little brother!'

'I beg of you, dear, not to allow this to make any difference in your behaviour towards Miss Palliser. She gave me no encouragement wilfully. And I'm not hopeless, Edie. Grace cares no more for Saxell than for me, and it would be best in my own interests to leave her for awhile, even if I could keep up appearances, which I can't. You will ignore all this ? You will not let her suspect anything of it?'

Edie promised.

Dunscombe entered the room the next day before Hugh was dressed.

'We cannot continue on these terms,' he said. 'Let us have an explanation.'

'I will give it you frankly, for I am going to the west coast of Africa for twelve months at least. Before you used words that could hardly be forgiven, I had heard remarks here and at Daneham which caused me to ask myself whether our intimacy was consistent with my honour. You had fallen into a habit of alluding to your admiration of my sister, and I had fallen into a habit of listening. At all times T have warned you that if need arose—there was no need and there is none now—but if it arose I warned you that my influence would be used against you. But that is not enough. There are matters of common report which compel me to take a stronger course, and therefore I was not sorry to have an opportunity of breaking off our former terms. You see that the case is beyond remedy.'

Dunscombe was white; his mouth quivered.

'May I ask,' he said, in a changed voice, 'whether you have transmitted these common reports to the ladies of your family?'

'I have not. But before I go I shall.'

Without another word, Dunscombe withdrew to his own house, and summoned Moore, his valet.

'Mr. Acland sent you a while ago to make acquaintance with Mr. Vane's clerk, What sort of man is he?'

'Mr. Davis is not a superior person, my lord. I should think he would be pleased to make himself useful for a trifle, if that is what your lordship means.'

'He is a respectable sort of man, of course?'

'Quite respectable, my lord.'

'And obliging?'

'Very obliging, my lord, I should say, when a matter is put before him with consideration.'

'And money?'

'That is what I mean, my lord.'

'Then find him this afternoon. I have some annoying business, which I would not ask my lawyers to conduct. If you are sure that Mr. Davis is trustworthy, bring him here.'

When Dunscombe returned to dress, the man was waiting. It is easy for one who leads a fast life to find work for a legal agent of the indefinite class. Dunscombe invited Mr. Davis to sit down, showed a number of letters referring to a claim which he desired to compromise, discussed the matter thoroughly, and offered a large percentage. Not till Mr. Davis rose to go did he say casually:

'It was my man who named you to me as an able and discreet adviser. I lent him to Acland on the occasion when he made your acquaintance. Moore guarantees your silence and trustworthiness in this case. You will not give a stranger the address of anybody concerned in *my* affairs?'

'Indeed I will not, my lord,' said Davis, much flurried. 'That was such a very trifling matter which Mr. Moore questioned me about.'

'Well, you will not forget that there are no trifles in my business ! By-the-bye, how does the claim of Major Saxell progress ?'

'It has come quite to a standstill, my lord. Mr. Vane has made up his mind that it will not hold water, as they say; and he is writing to India by next mail, advising Major Saxell to drop it.'

'This is very pleasant news! I am particularly interested in this case, not for the money question, but on account of some collateral issues that seem to arise. You understand me ?'

'I am not sure, my lord,' said Davis, with hesitation.

'It is not much of a secret that I admire Miss Acland,' Dunscombe replied steadily, but with an effort. 'Certain hints have reached me that cause a vague uneasiness. You understand now ?'

'Your lordship thinks that there is something which might influence him in the idea of marrying Miss Acland ?'

'Quite so.'

'Might I ask what those hints were ? Possibly I could relieve your lordship's mind.'

'Why,' said Dunscombe angrily, 'about Hugh's birth in the first place.'

'Mr. Hugh is legitimate—doubly so, I may say.'

'That's it!—there is a mystery. What was the date of Mrs. Acland's marriage?'

'In the latter part of 1857, nominally——'

'And he was born in February, 1858?'

'Allow me——'

'Your explanation is not enough. And what is the connection of Mrs. Acland with Julius Beaver?'

'As for that, my lord, I'm sorry to confess that we know nothing certainly. But Mr. Vane is quite satisfied with her refutation of the innuendoes made by Sergeant-Major Raikes.'

'In such a grave matter I cannot accept Mr. Vane's opinion any more than yours. Now, Mr. Davis, unless I have been misinformed, Raikes or Acland or Hardwicke, or whoever he was, preferred certain charges against the lady, which Vane most properly suppressed. I am deeply interested, as you perceive, in knowing what those charges are, and in ascertaining for myself the facts. It is needless to give you my word of honour that they will not be divulged. Could you obtain me a copy, or a sight, of the statements which Raikes made ?'

Davis hesitated no longer.

'It is a risk, my lord,' he said.

'You may name your own terms.'

'Your lordship wishes to marry Miss Acland, but before committing yourself you desire to learn the truth of certain scandals against the family. Very natural and proper, if I may be allowed to express an opinion.'

'I You are perfectly right.'

'Your lordship's confidence flatters me! But Mr. Vane, perhaps, would not acknowledge my right to assist you.'

'My gratitude shall be all the more substantial.'

'I might probably be dismissed !'

'Let me have those papers for half a day, and I will hand you three years' salary down on receipt.'

'That is enough ! A poor man, my lord, cannot always venture to follow a good impulse, however strongly his better nature may commend it to him. But assured against the consequences, he can give himself fair play. We are just now transcribing all the evidence on either side, to be sent to India, with Mr. Vane's remarks. By a little management and good luck, I might obtain possession of the documents your lordship wishes to see. But I beg you not to keep them more than half a day.'

'Have you read the things yourself ?' asked Dunscombe jealously.

'Not exactly, my lord. Mr. Vane keeps them locked up. But I have confidentially transcribed Mrs. Acland's answers, intended for Major Saxell personally.'

'So the case in itself falls to the ground?'

'Absolutely. Sergeant-Major Raikes was the Rev. Henry Hardwicke. as sure as I am James Davis and your lordship is——what your lordship pleases to call yourself.'

'Let me have a copy of Mrs. Acland's reply also, if possible. When Major Saxell drops the question, if he should, his claim passes to Mrs. Saxell, as I understand?'

'Yes, and she's an ugly customer, my lord. But so far as scandal is concerned, her son has written Mr. Vane to destroy all the matter he suppressed, before handing over the evidence, if Mrs. Saxell should begin proceedings; and Mr. Vane told me he would have done so on his own account, without authority.'

'That's rather a bold step, isn't it?'

'Very bold for a poor man, my lord. Mr. Vane would do it, if necessary, however. But the lady will not know these things, and if counsel ask about the mutilated diary the chances are that they can be satisfied without much trouble.'

'If the case is as plain as you describe, how could Hardwicke possibly have hoped to carry his fraud through?'

'Our case is that he didn't hope. In all the years he was writing slander against Mrs. Acland, and pretending to himself that he was her husband, Raikes never made a move. We insist a good deal on that. But when the game was up, and he la} T dying, it seems to have been a satisfaction to him to do something at last which would make matters unpleasant for those who survived him. And if Major Saxell hadn't been a chivalrous sort of a gentleman, Raikes would have succeeded with a vengeance, whether the Major gained his case or not. Your lordship will judge for yourself. Though it's all lies, a lady in the upper circles would have found an inquiry very unpleasant. Perhaps your lordship is not aware that he intended at one time to write all his story about her mother to Miss Acland—and most likely he did so!'

'No, by heaven! I had not heard that ! How do you know?'

'We found the rough draft of a letter addressed to her among the things at Meerut.'

'Was there a date? What did it contain?'

'It contained all the charges, put as black as possible. We judge that the date would be somewhere in 1878. Your lordship is agitated, naturally!'

'What an infernal scoundrel! This is worse than I ever thought.'

'If we hadn't stronger evidence,' said Mr. Davis, 'the fact that Raikes was a scoundrel would not prove him not to have been Acland, my lord.'

'Send what you have promised as soon as you can. Good-evening.'

The Codes Of Hammurabi And Moses
W. W. Davies

QTY

The discovery of the Hammurabi Code is one of the greatest achievements of archaeology, and is of paramount interest, not only to the student of the Bible, but also to all those interested in ancient history...

Religion **ISBN:** *1-59462-338-4* **Pages:**132

MSRP $12.95

The Theory of Moral Sentiments
Adam Smith

QTY

This work from 1749. contains original theories of conscience amd moral judgment and it is the foundation for systemof morals.

Philosophy ISBN: *1-59462-777-0* **Pages:**536

MSRP $19.95

Jessica's First Prayer
Hesba Stretton

QTY

In a screened and secluded corner of one of the many railway-bridges which span the streets of London there could be seen a few years ago, from five o'clock every morning until half past eight, a tidily set-out coffee-stall, consisting of a trestle and board, upon which stood two large tin cans, with a small fire of charcoal burning under each so as to keep the coffee boiling during the early hours of the morning when the work-people were thronging into the city on their way to their daily toil...

Pages:84

Childrens ISBN: *1-59462-373-2* *MSRP $9.95*

My Life and Work
Henry Ford

QTY

Henry Ford revolutionized the world with his implementation of mass production for the Model T automobile. Gain valuable business insight into his life and work with his own auto-biography... "We have only started on our development of our country we have not as yet, with all our talk of wonderful progress, done more than scratch the surface. The progress has been wonderful enough but..."

Pages:300

Biographies/ ISBN: *1-59462-198-5* *MSRP $21.95*

The Art of Cross-Examination
Francis Wellman

QTY

I presume it is the experience of every author, after his first book is published upon an important subject, to be almost overwhelmed with a wealth of ideas and illustrations which could readily have been included in his book, and which to his own mind, at least, seem to make a second edition inevitable. Such certainly was the case with me; and when the first edition had reached its sixth impression in five months, I rejoiced to learn that it seemed to my publishers that the book had met with a sufficiently favorable reception to justify a second and considerably enlarged edition. ...

Pages:412

Reference   **ISBN: *1-59462-647-2***   *MSRP $19.95*

On the Duty of Civil Disobedience
Henry David Thoreau

QTY

Thoreau wrote his famous essay, On the Duty of Civil Disobedience, as a protest against an unjust but popular war and the immoral but popular institution of slave-owning. He did more than write—he declined to pay his taxes, and was hauled off to gaol in consequence. Who can say how much this refusal of his hastened the end of the war and of slavery ?

Law   **ISBN: *1-59462-747-9***   **Pages:48**

MSRP $7.45

Dream Psychology Psychoanalysis for Beginners
Sigmund Freud

QTY

Sigmund Freud, born Sigismund Schlomo Freud (May 6, 1856 - September 23, 1939), was a Jewish-Austrian neurologist and psychiatrist who co-founded the psychoanalytic school of psychology. Freud is best known for his theories of the unconscious mind, especially involving the mechanism of repression; his redefinition of sexual desire as mobile and directed towards a wide variety of objects; and his therapeutic techniques, especially his understanding of transference in the therapeutic relationship and the presumed value of dreams as sources of insight into unconscious desires.

Pages:196

Psychology   **ISBN: *1-59462-905-6***   *MSRP $15.45*

The Miracle of Right Thought
Orison Swett Marden

QTY

Believe with all of your heart that you will do what you were made to do. When the mind has once formed the habit of holding cheerful, happy, prosperous pictures, it will not be easy to form the opposite habit. It does not matter how improbable or how far away this realization may see, or how dark the prospects may be, if we visualize them as best we can, as vividly as possible, hold tenaciously to them and vigorously struggle to attain them, they will gradually become actualized, realized in the life. But a desire, a longing without endeavor, a yearning abandoned or held indifferently will vanish without realization.

Pages:360

Self Help   **ISBN: *1-59462-644-8***   *MSRP $25.45*

www.bookjungle.com *email: sales@bookjungle.com fax: 630-214-0564 mail: Book Jungle PO Box 2226 Champaign, IL 61825*

QTY

The Rosicrucian Cosmo-Conception Mystic Christianity *by Max Heindel*   ISBN: *1-59462-188-8* **$38.95**
The Rosicrucian Cosmo-conception is not dogmatic, neither does it appeal to any other authority than the reason of the student. It is: not controversial, but is: sent forth in the, hope that it may help to clear...   New Age/Religion Pages 646

Abandonment To Divine Providence *by Jean-Pierre de Caussade*   ISBN: *1-59462-228-0* **$25.95**
"The Rev. Jean Pierre de Caussade was one of the most remarkable spiritual writers of the Society of Jesus in France in the 18th Century. His death took place at Toulouse in 1751. His works have gone through many editions and have been republished...   Inspirational/Religion Pages 400

Mental Chemistry *by Charles Haanel*   ISBN: *1-59462-192-6* **$23.95**
Mental Chemistry allows the change of material conditions by combining and appropriately utilizing the power of the mind. Much like applied chemistry creates something new and unique out of careful combinations of chemicals the mastery of mental chemistry...   New Age Pages 354

The Letters of Robert Browning and Elizabeth Barret Barrett 1845-1846 vol II   ISBN: *1-59462-193-4* **$35.95**
by Robert Browning and Elizabeth Barrett   Biographies Pages 596

Gleanings In Genesis (volume I) *by Arthur W. Pink*   ISBN: *1-59462-130-6* **$27.45**
Appropriately has Genesis been termed "the seed plot of the Bible" for in it we have, in germ form, almost all of the great doctrines which are afterwards fully developed in the books of Scripture which follow...   Religion/Inspirational Pages 420

The Master Key *by L. W. de Laurence*   ISBN: *1-59462-001-6* **$30.95**
In no branch of human knowledge has there been a more lively increase of the spirit of research during the past few years than in the study of Psychology, Concentration and Mental Discipline. The requests for authentic lessons in Thought Control, Mental Discipline and...   New Age/Business Pages 422

The Lesser Key Of Solomon Goetia *by L. W. de Laurence*   ISBN: *1-59462-092-X* **$9.95**
This translation of the first book of the "Lernegton" which is now for the first time made accessible to students of Talismanic Magic was done, after careful collation and edition, from numerous Ancient Manuscripts in Hebrew, Latin, and French...   New Age/Occult Pages 92

Rubaiyat Of Omar Khayyam *by Edward Fitzgerald*   ISBN: *1-59462-332-5* **$13.95**
Edward Fitzgerald, whom the world has already learned, in spite of his own efforts to remain within the shadow of anonymity, to look upon as one of the rarest poets of the century, was born at Bredfield, in Suffolk, on the 31st of March, 1809. He was the third son of John Purcell...   Music Pages 172

Ancient Law *by Henry Maine*   ISBN: *1-59462-128-4* **$29.95**
The chief object of the following pages is to indicate some of the earliest ideas of mankind, as they are reflected in Ancient Law, and to point out the relation of those ideas to modern thought.   Religion/History Pages 452

Far-Away Stories *by William J. Locke*   ISBN: *1-59462-129-2* **$19.45**
"Good wine needs no bush, but a collection of mixed vintages does. And this book is just such a collection. Some of the stories I do not want to remain buried for ever in the museum files of dead magazine-numbers an author's not unpardonable vanity..."   Fiction Pages 272

Life of David Crockett *by David Crockett*   ISBN: *1-59462-250-7* **$27.45**
"Colonel David Crockett was one of the most remarkable men of the times in which he lived. Born in humble life, but gifted with a strong will, an indomitable courage, and unremitting perseverance...   Biographies/New Age Pages 424

Lip-Reading *by Edward Nitchie*   ISBN: *1-59462-206-X* **$25.95**
Edward B. Nitchie, founder of the New York School for the Hard of Hearing, now the Nitchie School of Lip-Reading, Inc, wrote "LIP-READING Principles and Practice". The development and perfecting of this meritorious work on lip-reading was an undertaking...   How-to Pages 400

A Handbook of Suggestive Therapeutics, Applied Hypnotism, Psychic Science   ISBN: *1-59462-214-0* **$24.95**
by Henry Munro   Health/New Age/Health/Self-help Pages 376

A Doll's House: and Two Other Plays *by Henrik Ibsen*   ISBN: *1-59462-112-8* **$19.95**
Henrik Ibsen created this classic when in revolutionary 1848 Rome. Introducing some striking concepts in playwriting for the realist genre, this play has been studied the world over.   Fiction/Classics/Plays 308

The Light of Asia *by sir Edwin Arnold*   ISBN: *1-59462-204-3* **$13.95**
In this poetic masterpiece, Edwin Arnold describes the life and teachings of Buddha. The man who was to become known as Buddha to the world was born as Prince Gautama of India but he rejected the worldly riches and abandoned the reigns of power when...   Religion/History/Biographies Pages 170

The Complete Works of Guy de Maupassant *by Guy de Maupassant*   ISBN: *1-59462-157-8* **$16.95**
"For days and days, nights and nights, I had dreamed of that first kiss which was to consecrate our engagement, and I knew not on what spot I should put my lips..."   Fiction/Classics Pages 240

The Art of Cross-Examination *by Francis L. Wellman*   ISBN: *1-59462-309-0* **$26.95**
Written by a renowned trial lawyer, Wellman imparts his experience and uses case studies to explain how to use psychology to extract desired information through questioning.   How-to/Science/Reference Pages 408

Answered or Unanswered? *by Louisa Vaughan*   ISBN: *1-59462-248-5* **$10.95**
Miracles of Faith in China   Religion Pages 112

The Edinburgh Lectures on Mental Science (1909) *by Thomas*   ISBN: *1-59462-008-3* **$11.95**
This book contains the substance of a course of lectures recently given by the writer in the Queen Street Hall, Edinburgh. Its purpose is to indicate the Natural Principles governing the relation between Mental Action and Material Conditions...   New Age/Psychology Pages 148

Ayesha *by H. Rider Haggard*   ISBN: *1-59462-301-5* **$24.95**
Verily and indeed it is the unexpected that happens! Probably if there was one person upon the earth from whom the Editor of this, and of a certain previous history, did not expect to hear again...   Classics Pages 380

Ayala's Angel *by Anthony Trollope*   ISBN: *1-59462-352-X* **$29.95**
The two girls were both pretty, but Lucy who was twenty-one who supposed to be simple and comparatively unattractive, whereas Ayala was credited, as her Bombwhat romantic name might show, with poetic charm and a taste for romance. Ayala when her father died was nineteen...   Fiction Pages 484

The American Commonwealth *by James Bryce*   ISBN: *1-59462-286-8* **$34.45**
An interpretation of American democratic political theory. It examines political mechanics and society from the perspective of Scotsman James Bryce   Politics Pages 572

Stories of the Pilgrims *by Margaret P. Pumphrey*   ISBN: *1-59462-116-0* **$17.95**
This book explores pilgrims religious oppression in England as well as their escape to Holland and eventual crossing to America on the Mayflower, and their early days in New England...   History Pages 268

QTY

The Fasting Cure *by Sinclair Upton*   ISBN: *1-59462-222-1*   **$13.95**
In the Cosmopolitan Magazine for May, 1910, and in the Contemporary Review (London) for April, 1910, I published an article dealing with my experi-
ences in fasting. I have written a great many magazine articles, but never one which attracted so much attention... New Age/Self Help/Health Pages 164

Hebrew Astrology *by Sepharial*   ISBN: *1-59462-308-2*   **$13.45**
In these days of advanced thinking it is a matter of common observation that we have left many of the old landmarks behind and that we are now pressing
forward to greater heights and to a wider horizon than that which represented the mind-content of our progenitors...   Astrology Pages 144

Thought Vibration or The Law of Attraction in the Thought World   ISBN: *1-59462-127-6*   **$12.95**

by William Walker Atkinson   *Psychology/Religion Pages 144*

Optimism *by Helen Keller*   ISBN: *1-59462-108-X*   **$15.95**
Helen Keller was blind, deaf, and mute since 19 months old, yet famously learned how to overcome these handicaps, communicate with the world, and
spread her lectures promoting optimism. An inspiring read for everyone...   Biographies/Inspirational Pages 84

Sara Crewe *by Frances Burnett*   ISBN: *1-59462-360-0*   **$9.45**
In the first place, Miss Minchin lived in London. Her home was a large, dull, tall one, in a large, dull square, where all the houses were alike, and all the
sparrows were alike, and where all the door-knockers made the same heavy sound...   Childrens/Classic Pages 88

The Autobiography of Benjamin Franklin *by Benjamin Franklin*   ISBN: *1-59462-135-7*   **$24.95**
The Autobiography of Benjamin Franklin has probably been more extensively read than any other American historical work, and no other book of its kind
has had such ups and downs of fortune. Franklin lived for many years in England, where he was agent...   Biographies/History Pages 332

Name	
Email	
Telephone	
Address	
City, State ZIP	

☐ **Credit Card**   ☐ **Check / Money Order**

Credit Card Number	
Expiration Date	
Signature	

Please Mail to: Book Jungle
PO Box 2226
Champaign, IL 61825
or Fax to: 630-214-0564

ORDERING INFORMATION

web*: www.bookjungle.com*
email*: sales@bookjungle.com*
fax*: 630-214-0564*
mail*: Book Jungle PO Box 2226 Champaign, IL 61825*
or PayPal *to sales@bookjungle.com*

Please contact us for bulk discounts

DIRECT-ORDER TERMS

20% Discount if You Order
Two or More Books
Free Domestic Shipping!
Accepted: Master Card, Visa,
Discover, American Express

www.ingramcontent.com/pod-product-compliance
Lightning Source LLC
Chambersburg PA
CBHW080747250626
47162CB00010B/3050